Pointer to a Crime

A Chief Inspector Pointer Mystery

By A. E. Fielding

Originally published in 1944

Pointer to a Crime

Published by Resurrected Press

This classic book was handcrafted by Resurrected Press. Resurrected Press is dedicated to bringing high quality classic books back to the readers who enjoy them. These are not scanned versions of the originals, but, rather, quality checked and edited books meant to be enjoyed!

Please visit ResurrectedPress.com to view our entire catalogue!

For news and updates, visit us on Facebook! Facebook.com/ResurrectedPress

ISBN 13: 978-1-943403-11-0

Printed in the United States of America

Other Resurrected Press books in *The Chief Inspector Pointer Mystery* Series

RESURRECTED PRESS CLASSIC MYSTERY CATALOGUE

Journeys into Mystery
Travel and Mystery in a More Elegant Time

The Edwardian Detectives
Literary Sleuths of the Edwardian Era

Gems of Mystery
Lost Jewels from a More Elegant Age

Anne Austin
One Drop of Blood
The Black Pigeon
Murder at Bridge

E. C. Bentley
Trent's Last Case: The Woman in Black

Ernest Bramah
Max Carrados Resurrected:
The Detective Stories of Max Carrados

Agatha Christie
The Secret Adversary
The Mysterious Affair at Styles

Octavus Roy Cohen
Midnight

Freeman Wills Croft
The Ponson Case
The Pit Prop Syndicate

Whose Body?

Sir William Magnay
The Hunt Ball Mystery

Mabel and Paul Thorne
The Sheridan Road Mystery

Louis Tracy
The Strange Case of Mortimer Fenley
The Albert Gate Mystery
The Bartlett Mystery
The Postmaster's Daughter
The House of Peril
The Sandling Case: What Would You Have Done?

Charles Edmonds Walk
The Paternoster Ruby

John R. Watson
The Mystery of the Downs
The Hampstead Mystery

Edgar Wallace
The Daffodil Mystery
The Crimson Circle

Carolyn Wells
Vicky Van
The Man Who Fell Through the Earth
In the Onyx Lobby
Raspberry Jam
The Clue
The Room with the Tassels
The Vanishing of Betty Varian
The Mystery Girl
The White Alley
The Curved Blades

Anybody but Anne
The Bride of a Moment
Faulkner's Folly
The Diamond Pin
The Gold Bag
The Mystery of the Sycamore
The Come Back

Raoul Whitfield
Death in a Bowl

And much more!
Visit ResurrectedPress.com
for our complete catalogue

FOREWORD

The period between the First and Second World Wars has rightly been called the "Golden Age of British Mysteries." It was during this period that Agatha Christie, Dorothy L. Sayers, and Margery Allingham first turned their pens to crime. On the male side, the era saw such writers as Anthony Berkeley, John Dickson Carr, and Freeman Wills Crofts join the ranks of writers of detective fiction. The genre was immensely popular at the time on both sides of the Atlantic, and by the end of the 1930's one out of every four novels published in Britain was a mystery.

While Agatha Christie and a few of her peers have remained popular and in print to this day, the same cannot be said of all the authors of this period. With so many mysteries published in the period, it is inevitable that many of them would become obscure or worse, forgotten, often with no justification other than changing public tastes. The case of Archibald Fielding is one such, an author, who though popular enough to have a career spanning two decades and more than two dozen mysteries, has become such a cipher that his, or as seems more likely, her real identity has become as much a mystery as the books themselves.

While the identity of the author may forever remain an unsolved puzzle, there are some facts that may be inferred from the texts. It is likely that the author had an upbringing and education typical of the British upper middle class in the period before the Great War with all that implies; a familiarity with the classics, the arts, and music, a working knowledge of modern European languages, an appreciation of the finer things in life. The author certainly had also traveled abroad, primarily in the south of France, but probably to Belgium, Spain, and

Italy as well, as portions of several of the books are set in those locales.

The books attributed to Archibald Fielding, A. E. Fielding, or Archibald E. Fielding, are quintessential Golden Age British mysteries. They include all the attributes, the country houses, the tangled webs of relationships, the somewhat feckless cast of characters who seem to have nothing better to do with themselves than to murder or be murdered. Their focus is on a middle class and upper class struggling to find themselves in the new realities of the post war era while still trying to live the lifestyle of the Edwardian era. Things are never as they seem, red herrings are distributed liberally throughout the pages as are the clues that will ultimately lead to the solution of "the puzzle," for the British mysteries of this period are centered on the puzzle element which both the reader and the detective must solve before the last page.

A majority of the Fielding mysteries involve the character of Chief Inspector Pointer. Unlike the eccentric Belgian Hercule Poirot, the flamboyant Lord Peter Wimsey, or the somewhat mysterious Albert Campion, Pointer is merely a competent, sometimes clever, occasionally intuitive policeman. And unlike, as with Inspector French in the stories of Freeman Wills Croft, the emphasis is on the mystery itself, not the process of detection. The Pointer mysteries have a certain flair that separates them from the "humdrum" school of mysteries that were starting to appear at the same time. Stylistically, they fall somewhere between the works of Christie and those of Ngaio Marsh or E. C. R. Lorac.

Pointer is nearly as much of a mystery as the author. Very little of his personal life is revealed in the books. He is described as being vaguely of Scottish ancestry whose father was a Coast guardsman on the Devon coast.. He is well read and educated, though his duties at Scotland Yard prevent him from enjoying those pursuits. In an early book in the series it is revealed that he spends a week or two each year climbing mountains, his only apparent recreation, though before becoming a policeman he'd played football for the All England team. His success as a detective depends on his willingness to "suspect everyone" and to not being tied to any one theory. He is fluent in French, German, and Italian and familiar with those countries. He is, at least in the first two books, unmarried, and sharing lodgings with a bookbinder named O'Connor, in much the manner of Holmes and Watson, though this character is absent in the later works. One intriguing feature of the Pointer mysteries is that they all involve an unexpected twist at the end, wherein the mystery finally solved is often not the mystery invoked at the beginning of the book. *Pointer to a Crime* is no exception. Fielding introduces a number of red-herrings and subplots to confuse the reader while still largely playing fair with the reader. *Pointer to a Crime* begins with the brutal murder of a woman at a cottage called The Clearing in Lincolnshire. At first, only the local police deal with the crime, and there are no obvious suspects, at least none without alibis, but several aspects don't seem to fit the narrative of the crime and would appear to be senseless and without purpose. It is only when Pointer discovers a link to another case that he is working on, the apparent suicide of the owner of a chain of hair-salons, that a solution is discovered.

The publication of *Pointer to a Crime* raises almost as many questions as does the identity of the author. It is the twenty-third and final book to feature Chief Inspector Pointer, yet, though Fielding had written one or more books a year leading up to the second to the last book in the series, *Scarecrow*, published in 1937, seven years were to elapse until the publication of *Pointer to a Crime* in 1944. Was this due to reasons of health, the dislocations caused by the war, or perhaps a change in readership? Or had the author grown tired of Pointer? The latter is a possibility, as Fielding had published as the previous book, the only non-Pointer mystery, *Murder in Suffolk* in 1938.

Pointer to a Crime was published in 1944 in the middle of World War II, and war time conditions are reflected in several aspects of the story. One suspects that they also played a role in the production of the book. The proofreading of the original text seems more haphazard than usual, and the author's punctuation and grammar, always somewhat eccentric, seem even more so than in the previous books. Was this due to the fact that the more experienced workers at the publisher were involved in war work? Or, does it reflect a lack of involvement by Fielding in the process? Is it possible that *Pointer to a Crime* was a previously unpublished manuscript that had been hastily modified to include war-time references before being released in 1944? Is it even possible that *Pointer to a Crime* had been languishing in the publisher's offices since the 1930's and someone other than Fielding made some changes in order to fit the times? All this, is of course, idle speculation, and it is unlikely at this late date that these questions will ever be answered. It is left only for the reader to enjoy the book as it is.

Despite their current obscurity, the mysteries of Archibald Fielding, whoever he or she might have been, are well written, well crafted examples of the form, worthy of the interest of the fans of the genre. It is with pleasure, then, that Resurrected Press presents this new edition of *Pointer to a Crime* and others in the series to its readers.

DISCLAIMER: Wherever possible, this edition follows the punctuation and spelling of the original edition without modification except in cases of very obvious typographical errors. Resurrected Press debated whether to heavily edit during the proofing process, but determined that the reader should experience the same assortment of unusual sentence structures and punctuation as were included in the original volume of the book.

About the Cover:
The Cover has been reproduced based on the original cover of the book

About the Author
The identity of the author is as much a mystery as the plots of the novels. Two dozen novels were published from 1924 to 1944 as by Archibald Fielding, A. E. Fielding, or Archibald E. Fielding, yet the only clue as to the real author is a comment by the American publishers, H.C. Kinsey Co. that A. E. Fielding was in reality a "middle-aged English woman by the name of Dorothy Feilding whose peacetime address is Sheffield Terrace, Kensington, London, and who enjoys gardening." Research on the part of John Herrington has uncovered a person by that name living at 2 Sheffield Terrace from 1932-1936. She appears to have moved to Islington in 1937 after which she disappears. To complicate things, some have attributed the authorship to Lady Dorothy Mary Evelyn Moore nee Feilding (1889-1935), however, a grandson of Lady Dorothy denied any family knowledge of such authorship. The archivist at Collins, the British publisher, reports that any records of A. Fielding were presumably lost during WWII. Birthdates have been given variously as 1884, 1889, and 1900. Unless new information comes to light, it would appear that the real authorship must remain a mystery.

Greg Fowlkes
Editor-In-Chief
Resurrected Press
www.ResurrectedPress.com
www.Facebook.com/ResurrectedPress

CHAPTER ONE

"I always get what I want." Zilla Ash stretched her long arms and threw back her head. She spoke with conscious arrogance. "If I want it enough," she amplified, leaning back against the mantelshelf.

"I fancy you work a bit as well," her mother said skeptically, looking up from some canteen accounts that she was adding up, "and I'm afraid your methods won't always bear investigation."

"All done by kindness," protested Zilla, lighting a cigarette.

Her sister Margaret gave a laugh, and then, looking at the clock, rose with the help of a stick, and made for the door. She had hurt her foot badly while on ambulance work during the last air raid.

"Come along, Zilla, we shall be late for The Clearing," she urged.

Her mother frowned. "I wondered why you had taken the day off—" she still spoke to her older daughter, "but of course The Clearing!"

"Ah, The Clearing!" Zilla mocked.

Margaret opened the door hastily.

"I'm off for my bike. Don't be late, Zilla, our dramatic entrances when everyone has waited to the limit are a bit of a nuisance."

Zilla did not make a move to follow her, but, instead, began to pace from the fireplace to the open windows and back again.

Mrs. Ash let it go on for a few minutes then laid down her pen.

"Do stay still, or go on to the Robsons," she begged. "I've never seen a panther lashing its tail except in a film, but you remind me of the picture. Is everything all right between you and Percy?"

"If you think anything connected with that sweet child would make me lash my tail—you flatter him." Zilla's tone was contemptuous. "It's the other end of me that he affects—makes me want to yawn my head off."

"You didn't yawn much until you got him," said her mother. "You're acting very foolishly. You know how his mother is trying to break off the engagement. You make it only too plain you don't care for Percy. He hasn't been near us for nearly a month, and considering his leave is up in a few days' time," Mrs. Ash pursed her lips, "you're acting most foolishly."

"Mrs. Bramwell wrote to me about a fortnight ago. There's another letter from her this morning, I see," Mrs. Ash glanced at a couple of unopened envelopes on a table near her. "Some more, very well founded complaints about your treatment of her only and much loved son, I'm afraid"

Zilla said nothing, but Mrs. Ash saw the signs of temper in her face.

"What is this madness that possesses you, Zilla? Harold Robson can't marry you. He's no money of his own—"

"He has now!" Zilla spoke sharply.

"His wife has. Robson doesn't get a penny, as long as she lives. But, apart from that, he loves Annabelle—and, frankly, she's a much prettier and younger woman than you are, Zilla. Doesn't your intelligence tell you that if he loved her when things were going so badly, he's hardly likely to be less devoted now that a fortune has tumbled into her lap? Come, use your brains. Cut Robson out of your life, as I heard him ask you to do. You've brought off this very good engagement in spite of Percy's mother. Having got him—keep him!"

Zilla turned a cigarette between her slender, strong fingers and said nothing.

"I don't talk of any affection you have for Percy," went on Mrs. Ash. "Personally, I think it was the fact that his mother was against the match, and that he was all but engaged to the Lorrilake girl, that made you choose him. You always want what you can't get."

Zilla agreed, smiling a little, "Even poor Percy himself. He didn't want to get engaged to me one little bit."

"After all, he is far and away the best catch around here, and you're thirty next month," Mrs. Ash said.

Zilla looked at herself in the mirror. There were two quite opposite opinions about her looks. She herself rather agreed with those who thought her ugly.

In the mirror she saw her mother pick up a letter and open it. Suddenly Mrs. Ash gave a little cry. Zilla had been expecting this, but her mother at the same time held out a little square of print.

"He's married—married to Loveday Lorrilake! Special license—they're on their honeymoon—"

"Well, that settles that," was all Zilla said.

"You knew this about this?" demanded Mrs. Ash.

"I broke off the engagement a fortnight ago," Zilla said calmly.

"You did not! His mother writes that *he* broke it off, since you showed so clearly that you had no love whatever for him. And did not even condescend to explain to him, when he wrote you, about being out in a car in High Ford wood alone with a Mr. Robson"—Mrs. Ash was reading from the letter—"around three o'clock in the morning. She writes further that, as you gave no explanation—obviously there was no explanation but one to give. 'So my dear son, on my advice—'"

Mrs. Ash fairly threw the letter on to the table.

"Were you out at that time, and in that place, with Harold Robson?"

"I don't see that you have any right to ask me about it," Zilla said indifferently, "but, as a matter of fact, I was. I wonder how Percy and the old cat learned of it."

"If Robson was with you, then it was some scheme of yours," her mother went on. "You got him there by some crooked work."

"I picked him up as he was trudging blamelessly home in the blackout—missed the last bus," Zilla explained patiently.

"High Ford isn't on his way home, nor on yours," was the reply.

"I got lost," Zilla murmured with a grin. "But calm yourself. We spent the entire time, until I started the engine again, talking about the price of fodder, and agreed that it is cheaper for a farmer to sell his cream as cream, rather than have it made into butter—"

"Mrs. Bramwell writes here about Percy's ring that he gave you. Says Loveday wants it, as part of a set of emeralds the Bramwells are giving her. It was Mrs. Bramwell's own stone once, it seems."

"That's why I insisted on having that particular one for my engagement ring," Zilla said gaily. "I'll send it back when I'm ready. Not before."

Mrs. Ash put down the letter that she had been rereading.

"I hope you're satisfied with yourself," she said grimly. "You've lost Percy Bramwell on account of a man who doesn't care for you, and couldn't marry you if he did. How the neighborhood will chuckle at the broken engagement. You're not popular, you know, Zilla. And now, how about your getting everything if you only want it badly enough?"

Zilla turned on her heel.

"I never wanted Percy Bramwell, remember," she said through clenched teeth. "As for laughing—let people wait a bit!" and with that she swung out of the room and down the drive, her tall, beautiful figure flying over the ground as though whipped by some invisible lash.

Mrs. Ash turned to her accounts with relief. Thank Heaven she would not see Zilla again, until, evening. For once she did not even care that she was going to the Robsons' cottage. Zilla had sown, and would have to reap now. But who would have thought, mused the mother, that her showy daughter would prove so difficult to marry off?

It was an hour later when Mr. Ash came into the dining room, bringing with him a whiff of fresh summer air.

Mrs. Ash seated herself at the table, and began to study a pile of steaming potatoes in front of her. Then she caught sight of a few small pieces of meat under the mound, and, felt relieved. She fished for the best bits now, with an air of helping her husband to the first spoonful that came to hand.

"'The girls are out. Lunching at The Clearing today." She passed him the plate.

"Sounds funny," said her husband with a half-smile "Who'd have thought, a year ago, that the Robsons would be giving lunch parties—and at The Clearing, of all the dismal spots—as it was then." He opened a letter as he spoke, and skimmed through it—then he glanced at a little folder of views that went with it.

"It's from the hotel in Cornwall that I wrote to about our summer holiday. Sounds all right. In fact it winds up—" He began to read from the folder "You'll love it with us. So come and bring the dog."

"I wouldn't mind taking Rover with us," said Mrs. Ash.

"Rover's sold," said her husband, "good price too. The Robsons have bought him."

"Surely they're staying longer at The Clearing than they did last time."

"Only one day longer. Why?"

"I shall be glad when they've gone," Mrs. Ash spoke under her breath. "Zilla took a day off from her egg collecting at the farms on purpose to go to lunch."

"And why not?" her husband asked carelessly.

"When Zilla goes to The Clearing it isn't to see *Annabelle* Robson." Mrs. Ash stressed the first name.

Ash gave a snort of derision.

"As it happens, Robson's in Gainsborough till tomorrow. I saw him leave myself by the nine o'clock train. He told me he was off to Gainsborough to get some extra fodder allowances for his new cattle."

"Edward," Mrs. Ash said suddenly, instead of replying, "has it ever struck you that Zilla is unlucky?"

"Never thought about it."

"But do you think she is unlucky? Some people are," persisted his wife.

Ash considered for a moment. He seemed doubtful.

"Well, you know my theory that there's no such thing as bad or good luck. What people call that, is really bad or good judgment. As Zilla has no judgment whatever, I suppose you would call her unlucky. I should simply call her a very silly young woman. But what's happened now?"

"Percy Bramwell heard of some foolishness of hers and tried to get an explanation out of her so Zilla broke off the engagement." Mrs. Ash had no intention of telling what had really happened.

Ash looked only mildly interested.

"Well, he always seemed a very dull fish to me," he said. "Zilla could do much better. She's young yet."

To her father, the girl was barely out of the nursery. Mrs. Ash would have said as much, but at that moment the door opened and Margaret came in.

"I thought you were staying to lunch at the Clearing with the Robsons." The mother spoke in dismay. There had been a difficulty in stretching the stew for her husband and herself; there was nothing left for the daughter but bread and cheese.

"Nothing for lunch," explained Margaret. "We were to have had rabbit, but the cat got it first." Margaret laughed. "We ought to've had Rover there."

"Where's Zilla?" asked the mother.

"She didn't turn up. Isn't she here?" Margaret asked.

Mrs. Ash shook her head.

Mr. Ash sprang into the breach with the account of the sale of Rover.

"So I've beet wasting my breath cracking him up to Annabelle. I was going to ask for a rakeoff on the sale, if one resulted." Margaret began cutting bread for herself. "I said he was the best guard, and the best tracker, and the best—"

"The Robsons know all about him," said her father, "they saw him put through his paces at the show."

"How was Annabelle?" asked Mrs. Ash.

"A bit royal," said Margaret, with a look of mischief.

"To think of a little farmer's daughter from Australia pitchforked into all that money," her mother was quite dismal about it. "It's a pity Annabelle doesn't carry it off better. By the way, was her cousin, Mr. Whitehouse, there? I want to ask him to lend me his secretary to help with the canteen accounts."

"No, he and Mr. Green were both in Lincoln," Annabelle said. But the odd-looking organist—Acland— was hovering about The Clearing most of the time. Annabelle says he drops in almost every day when she's alone."

"When she's alone?" repeated Mrs. Ash questioningly.

"So Annabelle says. She can't bear him."

"Does Robson know?" asked Ash, frowning.

"She won't tell him. He might be very angry, Annabelle thinks."

"He might," agreed Ash dryly.

"How was she looking?" asked Mrs. Ash.

"Awfully pretty, and dressed quite charmingly—just as one would expect the heroine of a fairy tale to look."

"By Jove, it is a fairy tale right enough," Ash sighed. "And when her father dies, and Annabelle gets the lot, she'll be worth thousands more."

"Let's hope she doesn't think of it like that," Mrs. Ash protested warmly.

"I don't suppose she does," but Margaret spoke doubtfully. "She left home so young though. Married when I she was eighteen."

"A father is a father even so. I don't like this constant talk as though Annabelle Robson weren't content with what has already dropped into her lap, without always adding that she'll have such a lot more when her father, who's dying, I understand, is taken too."

"Sorry, darling," Margaret's young face flushed. "I didn't mean it like that." She caught sight of the clock and swallowed some cheese swiftly. "I must be off." She snatched up tin hat and gas mask, and was off.

"I wish Zilla were like Margaret," said Mrs. Ash.

They talked of other things till the simple meal was ended. Then a bell rang.

"Mr. Ash in?" they heard a man's voice ask. Ash went to the door and flung it hospitably open.

"Come in, Robson, and let us get you some lunch."

Harold Robson was a broad-shouldered young man, with thick, curly brown hair, and a face that spoke of life in the open air.

He declined the invitation to lunch, but took some coffee.

"I met the bloke in the train whom I expected to have to wait till this evening to see, and we finished the business there and then in the railway compartment. Quick work for once. What I've come about is Rover. I'll take him on to Windhill at once, leave him there, and get back to The Clearing before dark. That will save bother tomorrow."

Ash had no objections to the idea, and while Robson wrote out the check he went on out to the kennels.

"How do you find The Clearing looking?" Mr. Ash asked politely.

"Not bad for this time of year."

"I hear Mr. Whitehouse wants to buy it." Mrs. Ash was making conversation.

The Robsons had only very recently risen into her social circle.

"But we don't want to sell it. It's all sorts of associations for us, Mrs. Ash. Misery—for it was misery, at first, and then a fair pittance, and then this unexpected fortune dropping out of the blue. No; we'll never sell The Clearing. Ah, there's your husband." He rose, and walked out to meet Ash, who had a splendid red setter on a lead.

The two men stood talking about the weather and the newest rationing difficulties.

The telephone bell in the house behind them rang, as they finally turned towards Robson's car. Mrs. Ash came hurrying out. At sight of the two she stopped.

"Oh, dear! I thought you had gone, Mr. Robson! Your wife has just rung up for Margaret to come over at once and bring the dog."

Robson looked surprised.

"My wife wants the dog?" He was puzzled.

"Rover had far better start his life with you at the house where he's going to live," Ash put in firmly.

"Has she rung off? Didn't you tell her I was here?" Robson stepped back into the house.

"She didn't wait for a reply. She seemed in a great hurry." Mrs. Ash was puzzled too. "Has she a sore throat?" she asked.

"A sore throat? She hadn't when I left The Clearing early this morning. May I use your phone? Hello! Hello! Hello!" He rattled the receiver. There was no reply, though he tried several times.

"She must be out in the garden," suggested Ash.

Robson hurried out to his car.

"I'll run around at once with the dog. She may have seen a rat about. Whitehouse has been complaining about them." Robson got into his car, fastened the dog's lead to a window handle, waved to the two, and drove off.

Captain Tyrwhitt felt very bored today. Only one week of his sick leave lay behind him, five stretched ahead. When he had accepted his uncle's invitation to spend his leave in the heart of Lincolnshire, the fact that the uncle was the chief constable had weighed with him more than the thought of bracing air. But, so far, he might as well have staying with the rector.

Then he lifted himself up hurriedly from the long chair in the rose garden. Major Findlay was calling him, and calling him in a tone that suggested some really interesting piece of news.

"Something that may interest you, Geoff." His uncle was at the telephone now, putting a call through for his car to be brought around at once. Then he turned: "There's been a murder at the village of Thoresway near here. Lonely spot."

"Man or woman ?" asked Tyrwhitt.

"Woman. Young. A Mrs. Robson. Apparently there's a bundle of notes missing too, so it may only be a passing tramp. But some of the points the super mentioned just now sound queer. The killer tried to get the husband too, but only bagged his dog. Funny thing is the dead woman had just phoned a friend for the dog to be brought up to the house to her."

As his car swished over the gravel, the chief constable hurried out with Tyrwhitt to where a very efficient-looking woman driver, also in police uniform, was holding the door open for them.

"Superintendent Clarkson is waiting for us outside his police station at Curtain Lindsey. We're to pick him up there. Apparently it was the husband who found his wife's body," continued Findlay.

It took them a quarter of an hour to reach the village of Thoresway, and another five minutes to drive on to the police station which served for several of the hamlets.

Superintendent Clarkson was a thick-set, big, burly man, with a Lincoln accent as broad as his chest.

"We can drive up to the gate, but not to the door," explained the superintendent, getting into the major's car to take the lead, with his men following on bicycles. "It's a good way from here. Lies quite away from other houses."

As the car swung around first one bend, then another, the superintendent related the circumstances of the crime, as so far known.

"Name of the murdered woman is Robson—Annabelle Robson," Clarkson began. "She and her husband—Harold Robson—are young people. They've run a market garden at Thoresway for the last two and a half years, until Mrs. Robson unexpectedly came into a large fortune about six months ago. Upon which, as the wife couldn't stick The Clearing any longer, they let it to a cousin of hers—I'll tell you about him presently—and bought a fine place the other side of Grantham. They come back every quarter to see things are going on all right, and have a word with old friends. That's why they're here at the moment."

"What's the local reputation of the couple?" asked Findlay.

"Excellent in every way, sir. You can't get the better of Robson in a bargain. Now, as to the finding of the body. Over the phone, Robson told us he left The Clearing this morning to catch the nine o'clock to Gainsborough, seeing about some fodder rations. He expected to be away till tomorrow, morning.

"Mrs. Robson was expecting the delivery of a fur coat that she had ordered in Lincoln, and he left sixty pounds with her to pay for it. That money has gone—so Robson says. But to go back to his own movements. He went to Gainsborough by train but in the compartment he met the very man he wanted to see, so he did his business there and then, and took the next train back, stopping at Mr. Ash's to buy a red setter that had won all the prizes yesterday."

"Damn!" Findlay was turning over the purchase of that very dog in his own mind. He had been one of the judges.

"While he was there, Mrs. Robson phoned to Mrs. Ash asking for the dog to be brought to her. Robson says he could get no reply from her when he rang up immediately to find out if anything was wrong. He only thought of rats, about which his wife's cousin—he's the tenant—had spoken only the day before. Getting no reply over the phone, he took the dog with him, and drove very slowly— the dog had not been in a car before—up to his cottage. Everything seemed quiet as he got there. You can't drive to the door, but only a few feet from the gate. He walked up, calling his wife, thinking she was in the garden, as she hadn't answered the telephone ring. He had the dog on the lead, of course. The dog got his leg over it, so Robson stooped to put it right. As he did so, a shot came from his bedroom window. It missed him, but the dog was killed outright. A second shot went through Robson's hat. That part of Robson's story sounds most extraordinary. I sent Higgins over at once, sir, told Robson to do nothing, touch nothing, speak to no one, till Higgins got there, but to report if he heard any noises in the house."

"Amazing story. Tell me about Robson, where does he come from?" asked Findlay.

"He, and his wife, and the wife's cousin, Whitehouse, to whom they let The Clearing, are all from Australia. From Canberra."

"What brought them over here?"

"Robson's father came from Yorkshire originally. He went out to Canberra as a government plant doctor—or plant consultant. He was supposed be the best man in all Australia, so Mr. Whitehouse says. After the Robsons married, times were very bad in Australia, so Robson maintained what his father—dead by that time—had always maintain, that living is much cheaper over here in England than it is in Australia, and the Robsons decided to come over and start a sort of superior market garden, growing the kind of plants we don't have much of. After three years in South Wales, they bought The Clearing, a three-acre lot and a tumbled down bungalow, about three years ago. The weather was devilish that year, as you may remember, for gardeners."

"I do remember," said the major feelingly, "drought and late frost—and drought again."

"Well, the Robsons came in for all that. He gave up all idea of growing superior vegetables, and found he had his work cut out to grow ordinary kinds. But he's a real gardener and a worker! Both are that. Or were, while they had to be. Regular slaves to their two acres they were. Bent backs were all anyone ever saw of the Robsons as they labored from dawn till late evening. But even so, it wasn't paying them. And they took to telling the milkman to call only every other day. Baker the same— and never saw the butcher. Then this cousin of Mrs. Robson's blew in quite unexpectedly from Australia. It seems her parents wanted to know whether things were going well with the couple, and had asked him to look them up. He's Mr. R. K. Whitehouse, the writer—the son of the Honorable Henry Whitehouse, grandson of Lord Shipley. To tell the truth, we were a bit surprised to know that Mrs. Robson had any such relations. She's rather— well—anyway, to go on—after he came down, things went much better. A check from her people reached Mrs. Robson every week. Only a pound, but it made a difference. So did the cousin staying on. He likes us in Thoresway, and we like him. Pleasant gentleman in the mid-forties. And with his coming, we all began to see something of the Robsons for the first time. Of Mrs. Robson mostly, for Robson still worked on his fields all day long. And, I'll say at once, what everyone will tell you, that a more devoted couple was never seen than those two. She had eyes only for him and he for her."

"Wasn't he-called up? Oh no, of course, reserved occupation."

"That's it, sir, and she has a cranky right arm. About six months ago came a surprising turn." The superintendent was enjoying the telling—"Some distant relative of Mrs. Robson's mother died, and she, as next of kin, came in for all his money. It was close on a million after all death duties were paid. Mrs. Robson's mother made a will at once, leaving a third to her daughter, and two-third her husband for his life, with remainder to Mrs. Robson after his death. I know all this so pat," as he turned to the chief constable, "because, believe me, the village has talked of nothing else since news came."

"I do believe you, Clarkson," said the chief constable with a look at Tyrwhitt which made him chuckle.

"Mrs. Robson almost went off her head with joy and surprise. None of them had even heard of a relative who had made all the money in mines. Mrs. Robson didn't have long to wait for the first share-out, for her mother was run over on her way back after signing the will. The whole fortune comes to Mrs. Robson—I mean would have come—any day, as her father is dying—Bright's disease— Whitehouse says. Yes, Mrs. Robson seemed all set for a fine life, and now—much good it'll do her."

"What was she like to look at?" asked the constable.

"Quite young, with a mop of very light golden hair, dark brown eyes, thick black brows, and a bright complexion."

"Pretty?" asked the chief constable.

"Quite pretty, sir," replied Clarkson. "But common looking, and the last type you'd have expected to work as she did. She showed lately how she enjoys a good time. But, as I say, she had eyes for no one but Robson, nor he for her. This'll be an awful blow to him—supposing he wasn't the one to do her in, of course," he hedged in a more official voice.

"Love often means jealousy," threw in the chief constable. "Young husband . . . Pretty girl . . . husband comes back earlier than expected—"

"But in this case it would mean apparently losing two-thirds of all the money, coming to his wife sir."

"Who will get the father's share now, do you know?"

"We were talking that over while waiting for you, sir. Whitehouse comes in for all that. The third left to Mrs.

Robson, of course, may come to her husband—but he's lost the rest. And apart from their being so wrapped up in each other—lovers if ever I saw any—Robson's not the chap to be hasty, and lose a large fortune. Which is why I think—so far—he's ruled out as the murderer."

"Is the cousin—Whitehouse—at The Clearing, too?"

"When the Robsons come down, he stays at the inn—the White Hind. There's only one good bedroom at the bungalow. Robson put it in perfect repair, but didn't alter it in any way, except to add a bathroom, a greenhouse, a porch, and put in some plumbing. By the way, sir, over the phone Robson mentioned a farmer, Uthwatt, whom he had passed on the road, and who had heard the shots. Robson said he's there with him."

"Well, if Uthwatt is there, we'll get some sense out of it all." The chief constable turned to his nephew. "He's head A.R.P. warden, as it happens, and one of our best men. Nothing important would escape his notice."

"Here we are, sir—just getting to The Clearing."

The car had stopped, turned down a narrow lane which ran for some minutes between high hedges. At its end was a wooden gate opening on to a pretty garden. The house itself was not visible until you turned the first corner of the gravel path around some fir trees and undergrowth. Roughly the whole place was, Tyrwhitt thought, shaped like a liqueur bottle, say a bottle of Benedictine, the gate being where the cork would come, the house set in the deepest curve of one shoulder.

A constable met them; he had been standing where he could watch both the front door and the gate.

"Mr. Robson and Mr. Uthwatt are both still inside," he said to the superintendent.

As they stepped up to the house they all halted and sniffed. A most appalling reek, as of burnt flesh reached them.

"Good God! What's happened?" asked the constable of Higgins.

"Like that when I got here, sir. A leather coat burning in the kitchen boiler."

"We'll see that first," said the major.

The superintendent stopped a moment to post the police, who had followed on their own bicycles, to various points, while the other three men hurried to the source of the stench. It was easily located as coming from a small kitchen boiler.

A very well-dressed, youngish man stood in the doorway.

"Hello, Uthwatt," said the chief constable, shaking hands, "what the devil have you got in there?"

"Leather coat, Major. I hooked it out and poured a pail of water over it to prevent its being burned entirely while Robson telephoned the police."

"The coat had been well wet with paraffin," sniffed the chief constable. He turned to the superintendent. "Get a man to work the thing apart. We want every scrap of it saved. Buttons, tags and so on . . . have it put in this pail," he pulled one forward with his foot. "And now, Uthwatt, I take it that Robson is in there? Then where's the body?"

"In there," said the farmer, his face very grim looking at another door. "I don't envy you what you'll have to look at."

The little group entered a fair-sized living room simply, but comfortably, furnished, with a telephone own table near a window. Near it a woman's body dressed in a green frock and light silk stockings lay sprawled. The face was battered beyond recognition.

CHAPTER TWO

The men bent down and studied the dead body attentively. Even Tyrwhitt, fresh from Libya, was shaken by what he saw. The doctor told them later that the woman had been killed outright by the first blow which had been struck with a sharp instrument, such an instrument, in fact, as was standing in the fender—a blood-stained wood-chopper. That blow, a very violent one, had come down, full force, on the top of her head. Then her face had been battered out of all semblance to anything human by a large, heavy, flat, object—such as a coal hod standing in the fender beside the chopper— which must have been brought down several times, also with great force, on her face as it lay upturned. The superintendent motioned to one of his men to come closer with his camera.

Tyrwhitt gave the body another careful look. He did not think that it had been moved since death, the room, too, did not look to him as though any struggle had taken place in it. His uncle said something to him in a quick whisper. They would search the cottage while the photographs were being taken.

On this floor was but the one living room, with kitchen, scullery and outhouses behind it. Upstairs there was a large front bedroom, with a smaller bedroom beside it. Against the window sill of the larger room a Home Guard's rifle was leaning. A glance down the barrel, without touching it, showed that it had been recently used.

"Belongs to Mr. Whitehouse," said one of the constables, looking at the name plate on it.

"Barrel's still warm," muttered the superintendent. Otherwise there was nothing to detain them in the room. Some very expensive, toilet articles littered the plain dressing table—evidently Mrs. Robson's. A few well-worn books spoke of the man who usually occupied it.

The small but adequate bathroom opened out of this bedroom. It showed no sign of having been used since morning. The other bedroom was much fuller of furniture than the larger room. A glance inside the wardrobe showed that whoever used it had a large amount of well-tailored suits.

There was another door opening off the landing. It was locked, but the hinges suggested that any stout blow would send the door flying.

The police looked at each other. Someone might be hiding here. Without a word, Clarkson ran down the stairs, and could be heard asking someone, Robson evidently, for the key.

"I haven't got it. It's only a boxroom. My wife kept the key."

Clarkson came upstairs again.

"Found these in her handbag," he said, dangling a ring with three keys on it. One looked like the key to the house. One would probably be to the garage. One seemed the kind to fit the lock in front of them.

Opening the door with it, they saw a small boxroom without any window. A pile of cardboard egg boxes were heaped in a corner. At the farther end was a small, old tin trunk, with an equally shabby imitation leather suitcase on it. Both were mark A. R. and both were unlocked. The under one bore an Australian steamer label. In it were some articles of woman's clothing. They looked very worn and threadbare. The suitcase was empty.

They re-locked the door after them, and went downstairs to the living room—which now would be more properly called the room of the dead. The chief constable turned towards the room's other door, beside the one by which they had just entered. A raised eyebrow on his part, and nod from the others, told him that the husband was behind it.

"Ready?" asked the chief constable, who now threw it open.

Uthwatt, Robson and the constable were sitting at the very simple kitchen table. Robson's face was composed in spite of its pallor, but to Tyrwhitt the eyes showed that a real blow had been received.

"Do you mind telling again just what has happened, as far as you know it, Mr. Robson?" asked the chief constable.

"I don't mind anything," said Robson in his deep very masculine voice, "but it's difficult to know, where to begin." He paused for a moment, while Uthwatt said he would wait in the passage.

Robson sat frowning for a moment longer, then he quietly and clearly explained that he left The Clearing this morning, expecting to be away in Gainsborough about some fodder till tomorrow morning, but by chance he had met the man in the train whom he had not expected to see except after hours of waiting. He had finished his business before the train ran into Gainsborough, so he had taken the next train back, had picked up his car at Thoresway station, and driven out to Ing's Place, thinking he would drive the dog he had just bought on to Windhill, so as to save time on the morrow when Mrs. Robson and he intended returning to their new home.

While he and Ash were talking together, the telephone had sounded. His wife had just rung up, and asked if Miss Ash would bring the dog to The Clearing. He, Robson, tried to have a word with her over the telephone, but there was no answer to his ring. He thought his wife had gone out into the garden, so, taking the dog along, he had set off for The Clearing.

"Unfortunately," Robson passed his hand over his forehead, "unfortunately, as I had no idea there was any hurry, and as I had the dog with me, and he looked a bit unhappy, I drove very slowly, talking to him as I went along. I passed Uthwatt about half-way along, having trouble with his radiator. When I got to the gate, I took the dog on the lead, and walked up the gravel path, around the bend, to the front door. As I went, I called her name, telling her Rover was with me. There was no reply. That didn't surprise me, because, as I say, when she hadn't answered my ring on the phone, I thought she was in some corner of the garden, and you can't always hear a hail from the gate, if you're busy."

"But you can hear it in the house?" asked the chief constable.

"Ordinarily you can. I was making for the vegetable garden as there was no reply, when Rover got a leg over the lead. I stopped, and bent down to get things right, when there was a crack—and Rover pitched over. I—it sounds mad—but for a second, I didn't realize what had happened, and, knelt down beside him in a sort of daze, when there was a second shot. I knew then what was happening—and my hat was on the gravel beside me. I was lying flat by then. I wasn't capable of thinking, it was like a film, or nightmare, or anything that isn't real. The next moment, my wits came back, and I thought of my wife—in the house in there—with some madman. I shouted to her and rushed in—and found my wife dead— butchered—battered to that in there—" He shuddered.

"Frankly I don't remember clearly what I did next. I rushed through the house, found no one. Rushed down the garden to the gate, searching the bushes. Out in the lane, I met Uthwatt. He had heard my calls, and came to see if anything was wrong. We ran back to the house together." Robson stopped, and waited a moment to pull himself together. "There's nothing more to tell. Oh yes, we smelled a fearful stink, it had been there all the time, I suppose, and found a coat crammed into the stove. Uthwatt put out the fire. I rang up the police."

The chief constable said a word to Clarkson, and went out to speak to Uthwatt. Tyrwhitt went with him. He did not want to stay alone with the stricken husband.

Uthwatt was walking up and down the bricks of the passage with agitated steps.

"It's beyond believing?" he said, shaking his head "Makes no sense at all!" He then proceeded to give a very clear account of how, while he was waiting for the water in his radiator to cool—the fan-belt was slack—about halfway between Ing's Place and The Clearing, Robson had passed him, driving very slowly, quieting a red setter beside him who was looking a bit worried. Some minutes later, he had heard Robson calling his wife. Then came two shots—rifle shots—one immediately after the other.

He couldn't give the time between being passed by Robson and hearing him call his wife. He was very busy just then with his overheated car, but thinking, he would put it at about ten minutes to quarter of an hour. It would have taken Robson quite that time to have reached the cottage from where he had passed him, going at the slow rate at which he was driving. Uthwatt went on to say that when he heard the shots he thought it was someone, Mrs. Robson probably, firing at wood-pigeons or rabbits, until he heard more and much louder shout of *Annabelle! Annabelle!* in Robson's voice which now sounded to him a bit wild. And then, a few yard from The Clearing, as he hurried up to see if any thing was wrong, he nearly collided with Robson who was running out from the gate and shoutin,g "Stop him! Don't let him get away! Catch him!"

He, Uthwatt, knew that no one had passed him on the way, but evidently something was wrong and when Robson signaled to him to come along and made for his own front door again, Uthwatt had run beside him, gathering from some broken words that something terrible had happened.

In the living room he saw what that something was. He and Robson rushed through the house and garden without finding anyone. A rifle was leaning against the window frame of the bedroom, It was still there, as neither man had touched it.

The smell of burning leather was by this time getting insupportable, and when they hurried in the scullery—it was its own guide—they found a leather coat burning in the boiler stove. Robson nearly collapsed; he, and Uthwatt too, had feared some horrible sight. He, Uthwatt, stayed in the scullery throwing water into the stove, while Robson telephoned for the police. Then the two men again went over the house. They had just finished when the village constable arrived.

The chief constable went back to Robson.

"Have you any theory—or idea—or guess as to the murderer?' he asked.

"Only this. When I last saw my wife—alive—she put a wad of some sixty pounds I had just given her on the table there in the living room. Right by the window. Someone from Lincoln was calling with a fur she had ordered, which Mrs. Robson wanted to wear back to our home. I don't know the shop's name. Any tramp could have seen it from the gravel path around the house—and if a tramp did, and my wife caught him at it—" Robson made a sort of gesture with one hand.

"But the brutality of bashing her face in?" Robson covered his own with his hands, and made no reply.

"And your own attempted murder?" asked the major.

"Got the wind up when I came along, and tried to gain time. If he had got me, no one would have known what had happened till tomorrow, or possibly, Monday."

"You didn't hear anyone moving about the house when you came in?"

"When I saw my wife—like that—I don't think I was capable of hearing a bomb go off," Robson replied hoarsely.

Tyrwhitt turned to the chief constable.

"I'll take another look at the living room," he said.

Back in the living room where a policeman stood on duty, he stood for a moment, looking about him. As requested, he pulled his gloves on, then stepped from object to object about the room. There had been no struggle, he felt sure. There was a larger table set to one side on which was covered typewriter and a litter of paper. A roll top desk—locked—with other paper on top. Books were plentiful. Books on the English countryside, its wildflowers and birds chiefly. Novels from a town circulating library. Newspapers from Australia . . . the usual jumble of any much-used room.

He carefully studied the figure lying there in its horrible condition. There was no sign of any struggle about it either. Curious that there had not been.

The major had now come in. He motioned for the constable to leave them alone.

"I suppose Robson has no doubt that this is Mrs. Robson?" Tyrwhitt asked.

"We've pressed him about that just now," Major Findlay said. "Of course a man would know his own wife—color of hair, and build, and so on, but Robson tells us that she had her right ear pierced twice—the first hole was too near the edge of the lobe."

They bent over the body. One ear lobe showed two small holes—not recently made.

Clarkson came in.

"It was the firm of Mount and Smith—from whom Mrs. Robson was going to get that fur coat. They haven't been here. They say that they phoned her to say that they would be sending it out first thing on Monday morning to Windhill. Mrs. Robson had answered the phone, but seemed in a rare hurry."

"Had they ever spoken to her before?" asked Findlay.

"Never, sir," replied Saunders. "That's just it—was it Mrs. Robson?"

"Another woman?" queried the major softly. "What could be the motive for that batering?" he asked under his breath. "Drunken fury, Robson suggests. There's evidently no question of hiding identity here."

They went into, the kitchen again.

"Was Mrs. Robson expecting any visitors this morning?" Findlay asked.

"Yes, the two Ash girls. They lunched here."

Clarkson asked him if he would step back into the living room for a moment, and, without touching any object, see if anything were missing, or out of place.

Robson looked about him quickly. No, he said, he could see nothing either missing or out of its usual place.

Clarkson held up a rusty chain, with an open padlock dangling from it. He had just caught sight of the gleam of metal in an armchair between cushion and back.

Robson eyed it as though puzzled.

"Belongs to Whitehouse, I fancy. Unless—" he looked at it closer. "We used to have that sort of thing for fastening small crates. In which case it was probably in one of the outhouses, or in the scullery somewhere. I think I can see how it got here—" he finished. "Mrs. Robson had asked for the dog to be brought over—this would probably be to fasten him up for a while."

The local ambulance now drove up. The body, covered with a sheet, was transferred to it quickly, and the car drove off.

Tyrwhitt continued his investigation of the room. Last of all, he picked up the telephone instrument which had already been tested for fingerprints and photographed. Finally he turned it over to inspect the baize bottom. He was looking for possible bloodstains, but it was something white instead that caught his eye. In what looked like a slit, made some time ago, a white button had caught; a white bone button sewed, as he found on taking it carefully out, to a piece of thick, tan leather—just such leather as now lay blackened and burnt beside the stove in the scullery. The little fragment might have explained everything could it only speak, Tyrwhitt thought. This piece had come from the neck of the garment. The stitching was strong and coarse, so was the thread with which the button had been sewn. There were tiny specks of what looked like blood on it.

He rejoined the others, who were talking to Robson and discussing that very coat.

"That leather coat being burnt was Mrs. Robson's?" his uncle said to him as he came in.

"We've all seen Mrs. Robson in it many and many a time," said Uthwatt, and Clarkson nodded agreement.

Robson had turned white under his tan.

"Sorry'," he mumbled, "just give me a minute—" he turned, and faced them again, openly wiping his eyes. "Sorry, but it somehow brings it home—yes, my wife always wore that coat when working on the place. I suppose she had it on this morning gardening . . . probably burnt it herself. It was shabby, and she was getting a bit sensitive about old garments—anything that didn't square up with our changed circumstances—"

It was at that moment that Tyrwhitt saw a face watching them from out of the clump of tall rhododendron opposite, the face of a young woman, dark-eyed, dark-haired, who was evidently standing on a bank running just outside the garden. In her concentration she did not seem to have eyes for anyone but Robson.

Robson was facing the window which gave on to the bushes, and so was facing her. But his eyes passed over her as though they did not see her.

The superintendent, who had also caught sight of her, stepped out on to the path, calling "Miss Ash, a moment! Miss Ash!"

The face vanished from the branches. The superintendent gave a shrug "We'll have a word with her later. That's Miss Ash," he added unnecessarily.

They stepped back into the room, where the chief constable was now questioning Robson about money matters

"No, the notes haven't been found, and of course may, as you think, be the motive for the murder. But also, they may have been taken merely as a blind. Do you mind explaining how your wife's legacy stands now?"

"My mother-in law left one-third of the money she inherited so unexpectedly to my wife, or rather the life interest of it, with reversion to our children, if any. Whom failing, it comes to me absolutely. The interest on the remaining two-thirds went to my wife's father, and on his death—he's not expected to last many days longer, the money would have come to my wife had she outlived him As things are now, I suppose, or rather I know, it all goes to the next of kin in the Bigger family, that means to Whitehouse, my wife's cousin on her mother's side, who is our tenant in this house."

"And where is Mr. Whitehouse at this moment?"

"He went in to Lincoln this morning, together with Green, his secretary. They ought to be back any time now. They're staying at the inn while we're here."

A telephone inquiry to the inn told the police that the two gentlemen in question had left around eleven that morning for Lincoln, and were expected back any time in the afternoon

"Now, Mr. Robson," the chief constable asked, turning again back to the room, "what are your own immediate plans?"

"What do you suppose?" asked Robson quietly. "The only thing I want in life is to find the man who did that, of course "

"We shall welcome any help," said the major politely. Robson did not reply.

"Take it from me," Findlay, went on in a kindly tone, but with a keen glance at him, "however much you want to be of use, professionals are best at this kind of thing. Help us, yes, but don't keep things from us with the idea that that way you will get quicker results."

Robson gave a noncommittal nod but did not speak

"Can you hand us over this house for the time being?"

"If my tenant doesn't mind. I don't know how I stand legally with regard to him—"

"It'll only be a question of him and his secretary staying on at the inn for tonight, and tomorrow morning," Findlay said.

Robson looked all in. "Do what you like with the cottage, as far as I am concerned, I shall stay at the inn too. I shall have to go back home at once, and probably on to London to see to some urgent matters—I must stop some purchases which it will now be quite impossible to complete. My wife was counting definitely on the rest of her mother's money coming to her very shortly indeed The last message we had from Canberra was that her father couldn't possibly last the week. As I say, I must tell the various people concerned at once that my—our—plans are off. But I'll be back tomorrow morning."

A constable was left to spend the night in the place and the chief constable led the way out, after Clarkson and he had given very careful instructions as to collecting and posting to the laboratory all the burnt parts of the coat found in the stove. Tyrwhitt handed over the button found under the telephone, which matched the half charred ones of the coat. Uthwatt had left some time previously.

"I'll go over to Ing's Place and have a word with the Ashes," Major Findlay said "Come along Geoffrey. Coming, Clarkson?"

He and the superintendent climbed in the police car, and drove off.

"I hope Mr. Whitehouse has a really good alibi," said the latter. "He seems a straightforward bloke—we all like him, but of course, he stands to benefit enormously. But if he's the chap—he'll give us a run for our money—you bet! He's a highbrow all right."

"Anything known against him besides that?" Tyrwhitt asked.

"Worst thing I know about him" acknowledged the superintendent, "is that he is so much with Green, his secretary. Green is a crooked stick, or I'm a Dutchman."

"There's one thing, in a small place like this, one won't need to break the news. Miss Ash'll have heard all about the murder as soon as we did—by Village Wireless," said the major.

"Family wireless in this case, sir," and Clarkson told him of Zilla Ash's face looking through the rhododendrons.

As a matter of fact, Ash had returned to his house a few minutes before, coming in with a very set face. His wife looked up in surprise.

"The boys?" she asked tensely. "Ambrose?—Vincent?"

"No, no! Nothing to do with them, or any of us. It's about Annabelle Robson."

"About Annabelle Robson!" she spoke in a tone of relief. "Now what's wrong? Doesn't she like the dog?"

"She's dead," her husband replied in a low voice.

"Dead?" Her tone was bewildered. "Dead!" she repeated incredulously. "Who told you?"

"One of the ditchers, but it's all over the place. Found dead by her husband. As a matter of fact found— murdered."

The next few minutes were spent in answering Mrs. Ash's questions and exclamations.

When both had more or less talked themselves out, there was a pause.

It was the husband who spoke first.

"Too bad the girls had to go in and see Annabelle— today of all days."

"Yes, it'll be ever so much more of a shock to them," said the mother.

"I was thinking of the police," Ash said. "They're bound to question them."

His wife stepped to the house door as she heard a bicycle on the path.

"Margaret, have you heard?" she called out. Margaret Ash had.

"They say in the village it's murder, mother," she spoke indignantly. "What won't people make up next!"

"Here's the police car! Turning in here! Damn!" said her father, fervently. "Keep out of things as much as you can, you two."

He stepped forward swiftly as a policeman got down to open the gate.

"I hope you won't mind us asking a few questions," said Major Findlay pleasantly, shaking hands, and introducing his nephew.

"Only anxious to be of any use," said Ash to that, leading the way in and asking them all to be seated.

"First of all, will you tell us about the sale to Mr. Robson of a dog that he says he took up with him to The Clearing today?" asked Finlay.

Ash gave a short, accurate account of the transaction "Robson told me today, when he came for the dog, that he had never intended taking him to The Clearing. It was arranged that the dog should be fetched by the Robsons early tomorrow and taken on to his new home. But, Robson turned up unexpectedly around midday today," Ash repeated what the men had already heard about the business having gone through so quickly, and about Robson's idea to take Rover home at once, so as to be able to drive home in greater comfort tomorrow.

"Was Mr. Robson in a hurry to get back to The Clearing?"

Ash looked puzzled.

Clarkson explained "It's an old trick for a jealous husband to let his wife, and friends, think that he's coming back at a certain time, and return hours before he is expected."

Ash rejected the idea in this case with firmness.

"Robson wasn't in a hurry to get back, quite the other way around," he said "It was I who was in a hurry. He rather wanted to mark time. Wanted me to show him some of my pigs. No, Robson wasn't in a hurry to go to The Clearing, that I'll swear. He was going off with Rover to their new place, not far from Grantham. It was only the telephone message his wife sent that made him drive there. She asked for the dog to be brought over at once."

The chief constable said that they would, of course, want an account from Mrs. Ash as to what were the exact words used, as the message was all important, being apparently sent just before Mrs. Robson's murder.

"I wish we knew why she wanted the dog," said Major Findlay. "In view of what happened, that was a very significant request. Looks as though she heard something moving about the house."

"Y-yes, but there's this," Ash filled his pipe reflectively. "What if she wanted to steal a march on her husband and get her own way about the dog coming first to The Clearing? Mrs. Robson was a bit like that, of late. Since she came into that money she liked to fling her weight about a bit, or let's say that, nowadays, when she wanted a thing a certain way she intended to get it done that way," he added. "Wish Margaret had stayed. The murder wouldn't have happened then."

"Oh? Why are you so sure she wouldn't have been murdered as well?" asked Tyrwhitt.

Ash seemed a little taken aback.

"I never thought of that! God, what an idea!"

"Were husband and wife on good terms with each other, would you say?" asked Findlay.

Ash's eyes met his squarely.

"The best. Never met such a devoted couple. And to have passed through the hard times they did, that means something."

A tap came on the door, and Mrs. Ash, with Margaret, entered. There were introductions. As they sat down, Mrs. Ash explained that her daughter had been into The Clearing only a little while before lunch, and, as the police would probably want to ask her about it, Margaret thought she would like to get it over.

Margaret was pale still from the shock of the news, but she spoke very simply and in a straightforward manner. She had run in to see Mrs. Robson this morning, because they were leaving next day, and it would be the last time that she and Annabelle Robson could have a chat. She had stayed about an hour, and then had gone on home. As to what they had talked about, she said that, among other things, Mrs. Robson had spoken of rats in the house, and had said that she was going to speak to Mr. Whitehouse about getting a well known vermin destroyer.

"Did she seem very, worried about the rats?" asked Major Waters.

Margaret said that Mrs. Robson had only referred to it quite casually.

"You and Mrs. Robson were great friends?" Findlay asked next.

Margaret hesitated.

"Not quite that. It was only after Mr. Whitehouse turned up, and she was able to take life a little easier, that we met at gas practice and ambulance drill. She inherited all that money soon after, you know, and since then, the Robsons have only been down here twice. Once in each quarter."

"You found Mrs. Robson quite as usual this morning? Knowing what has happened, thinking back now again very carefully, do you still think that everything was just as usual?" Findlay persisted.

"I do. I do," said Margaret very earnestly. "We talked of this and that—her new house, and what she was going to buy for it—Annabelle never was one to have much to say except about herself. She said how bored she was down here—didn't think she and her husband would keep up the quarterly visits. Mr. Whitehouse would have it all quite well looked after. She suggested our running into Lincoln when I first came, but when we looked up the trains, they didn't fit, so we dropped it. Besides, I didn't much want to go. I shall never forgive myself," Margaret added suddenly and her eyes were troubled.

Her mother made little comforting sounds, and reaching out, her father laid his lean brown had over his daughter's for a second.

"You said you looked up the trains? In what?" Tyrwhitt asked.

"In an A.B.C."

"Where is it usually kept?" he asked her.

"I found it this morning on the table by the window."

"And where did you leave it?" he asked again.

"Where I found it," was her reply.

"Was it a new one?"

"No, an old issue."

"Any marks on it?"

"Big old red ink stain on the top cover."

"Now about the dog!" the major said next. "Did you talk of him at all?"

"Mr. Robson said that her husband wanted a gun dog, and so she thought he couldn't do better than buy Rover. She didn't seem to care, one way or the other, so I cracked up Rover's points."

"Did she seem keen on the dog?" Clarkson asked.

"She wasn't keen on anything at all. Bored stiff down here. No, she just listened while polishing her nails. I only talked for the sake of saying something."

"Which of you suggested going into Lincoln?" asked the chief constable.

"She did. Just by way of doing something."

"Do you think she meant to be home when her husband returned?" was the next question. Margaret gave him a surprised look.

"I think, so," she said guardedly.

"I understand that she and her husband were devoted to each other?" said the chief constable.

"Very much so," she replied instantly.

"Up to this morning?" Tyrwhitt queried.

"I don't think there was any difference as to that," she replied "Simply as I say, Mrs. Robson has been so changed by her good fortune that one can't—couldn't—be so sure of anything—"

"Did she talk to you this morning about her husband at all?" he continued.

"All the time, more or less."

"Affectionately?"

"Well—she was fed up with his still being so keen on economy when there was no longer any need for that, as her father couldn't last the week. They knew that for certain."

The chief constable gave her a very keen look.

"Not much of a devoted daughter about that remark," he suggested.

"She never pretended to care much for either of her parents, but she said that she didn't intend to turn into an actress about her feelings. That a lot of girls felt the same way as she did, about their homes."

"She used to speak very differently from that," murmured Mrs. Ash, "when Mr. Whitehouse first arrived. She told me herself how fond of her mother she was . . . how she hoped she and Mr. Robson could go back for a visit to her old home. I'm afraid money does alter people. Often."

"Did her appearance change?" asked Tyrwhitt carelessly.

That battered face—could there be some clever substitution, after all?

Both women said that beyond improving her looks, Mrs. Robson had not altered at all.

"Had she any marks on her?" asked the superintendant.

"Yes," said Margaret promptly. "There are two marks like dots on the back of her left hand where she fell on a branched piece of wood some time ago. It's healed, but it left the marks. I saw them only this morning."

The three men facing her had seen them even later still.

"Oh, and then there was the right ear. She had had her ears pierced for earrings when she came back for the first time after she left The Clearing, and the hole wasn't centered properly. She had it drilled a second time. You could just see the first little dot, and she said she could feel it when she pinched the ear lobe."

The chief constable asked her if she would mind coming back with him in his car, and showing him where she had sat, where Mrs. Robson had sat, where she had put the railway guide, and so on.

Seeing the look on Ash's face, he said the room was quite tidied up now, and he would very much like her to do this, as it would help the police to get a grasp of the interview. Then he asked her when she left The Clearing.

Margaret was not at all sure. Around one, more or less. She had really had to tear herself away, as Mrs. Robson was so much at a loose end, that she couldn't bear to be left alone.

"You don't think she was afraid?"

"I'm sure she wasn't," Margaret said very firmly. "You can't be bored, and be afraid, at the same time, can you? And, as I say, she really was very bored. So much so, that when I left she said she was going to see if she could track the rats that she had heard moving overhead in the night. Said it would at least give her something to do. I thought it very amusing at the time, but—" she gulped, "her phone call for me—I wish I felt sure that she didn't come on someone hiding in the house, and that if I had stayed—" she did not finish.

"Now, Miss Ash," the chief constable turned to her.

"Mrs. Robson's telephone message is very important indeed. Will you tell us exactly what was said?"

She did so.

"Are you quite sure it was Mrs. Robson speaking?" pressed the chief constable.

She hesitated

"Well, since I know what has happened. I'm not so sure that it was Mrs. Robson. I may be quite wrong—" Mrs. Ash began to hedge.

"Probably are," said her husband gruffly. "You thought it was Annabelle Robson all right when you heard her. It's just thinking over this murder makes you imagine things"

"Of course when the voice said, 'Is that you, Mrs. Ash, this is Annabelle Robson speaking'—I took it that it was she. But since then—even at the time I thought that I should never have recognized the voice if she hadn't given her name. For one thing, she spoke all of a rush—and you know how Annabelle drawled," she added to her husband.

"She calls speaking in a rush 'common'," murmured Margaret, who could not yet think of the young woman as dead.

"And I noticed, even then, that the voice sounded much 'commoner' than Annabelle's usually did—there, I've used her pet word! I'm beginning to wonder if it was her at all."

"Of course it was!" said Ash impatiently. "She got the wind up over some noise she had heard—whether rats or not—and that would make her speak quickly, and as to sounding common—Annabelle's refinement never struck me as being more than skin deep."

"Maybe you're right," murmured his wife.

"And maybe you're right, Mrs. Ash," said Superintendent Clarkson with a faint smile.

"But if not Annabelle Robson, why should anyone want to fetch witnesses to The Clearing?" asked Ash. "And a dog—a really nasty customer if there was dirty work going on. Doesn't make sense."

"I think Miss Ash should be careful not to go about in solitary places till all this is settled up," the chief constable said slowly. He thought it possible that the girl was in danger from that telephone call. "By the way," he asked easily, "did Mrs. Robson ever wear a leather coat?"

"In the old days she fairly lived in one," said Margaret promptly. "Long before I ever spoke to her, when she was just a figure working from morning to night in the fields, I used to know that coat. Why?"

"Do you know where she keeps it?" Findlay asked.

"Has she another? She gave the old one to my sister. My sister's coupons were all used up, and she was very glad of it to wear when handling egg cases.

"Do you know where Miss Ash keeps hers?' asked Findlay.

"I don't think she has it any more. I think she wore it out. But I don't know for certain. Why?' Margaret asked.

"Can we have a word with Miss Ash?" asked Findlay next, but he was told the older daughter was not in though today was her day off.

"Mrs. Robson didn't ask her to lunch with you?" asked Findlay.

He was told that Zilla had been asked, but had apparently changed her mind at the last moment and had not gone.

"Will you ask her to ring me up when she gets in, I'd like a word with her," Findlay said easily, then he turned to Margaret again.

"Could you come back to The Clearing with us, and see if everything is as you last saw it?"

CHAPTER THREE

The drive to The Clearing was a silent one. At the gate a constable stepped forward.

"There's been a visitor here, sir. You gave orders that everyone was to be admitted who wasn't obviously a mere snooper. Some bloke by the name of Acland."

"Who's he?" Findlay asked Clarkson.

"Local reporter and organist."

"Where is he?"

"He had a word with Robson, then went off."

"Are the two—this Acland and Robson—good friends?" Findlay asked Clarkson, who had no idea on the subject.

Tyrwhitt held the front door open for Margaret. She stepped in with a fearful glance around the little hall, as though she expected to see portions of the late owner lying in the corners, but when Robson stepped out of the kitchen to meet them she went forward quickly.

"Harold!" Her two hands were extended. He grasped them tightly.

"Don't!" he said brokenly. "Don't! I know what you want to say—and thank you—but don't say it. You've come to tell about your talk with Annabelle this morning, I suppose? I'd like to hear every word too—if I may. She hoped you'd spend the day with her."

"I wish I had!" Margaret said again in self-reproach

"May I hear what she has to say?" Robson asked the chief constable.

"Do," said Findlay cordially, and Robson followed the little group into the room.

Margaret swiftly repeated her account of the morning's talk with the dead girl.

"Where did you leave Mrs. Robson? At the front door?" Findlay asked when she had finished

"No. At the garden gate."

"Did you see at any time a bundle of pound notes?" asked Robson

"A thick bundle with a rubber band around? It lay there on the desk, as far as I remember. Yes, I feel sure it did, for I had to move them a little to get space for both of us to see about the trains to Lincoln."

"Would you mind getting out the A.B.C. again?" Tyrwhitt asked.

She glanced at a shelf just beside the door into the passage. Some books were lying on it. She went and fingered them. Then she looked around the room.

"Here's where the A.B.C. was, and where I put it back when we'd looked up the trains."

"It's where it's always kept," added Robson, "what's this about your looking trains up in it?"

"Only as far as Lincoln," said Margaret. "Evidently it's been put somewhere else for the moment."

"I hope it hasn't got mixed with our papers," said Clarkson "Any name on it?"

Robbson did not think there was. It belonged to Whitehouse, his tenant, he said. There was red-ink stain half across the cover.

They all looked for it—without finding it.

"Anything else you miss?" Findlay asked her.

"Mrs. Robson was getting a book ready for the mail when I got here, she put it on the mantel by the clock. I meant to post it for her when I left, but I quite forgot it. She must have taken it down herself."

"About half an hour's walk there and back for her?" asked Clarkson.

"Quite. Mrs. Robson never walked fast."

"Wouldn't it go in the letter box at the cross-roads?"

"Too thick a book."

"Did you see the address?"

Margaret did not remember it.

"She wrote a line in the flyleaf, and I helped her find some brown paper and tie it up. She made beautifully neat parcels. But then, she was very neat in anything she did with her hands."

"Left-handed, wasn't she?" asked Clarkson.

"Only for a time, when she crushed her right arm in the gate one day," explained Robson. "But the arm was quite all right later."

Clarkson said a word to the chief constable and picked up the telephone. He dialled the post office.

"Did she use a blotter for what she wrote in the book, or on the cover?" asked Tyrwhitt.

"She used a white half-sheet which was lying on the blotter for what she wrote on the flyleaf. The package she blotted on the pad itself."

The police had not found any loose sheet, and there were no ink marks whatever on the blotting pad.

"Was the top of the blotter as it is now or had it been used?"

"It had been very much used. Mrs. Robson got some ink from her fountain pen on her fingers and rubbed it off on the blotter, or rather on the half-sheet that she used in the book."

Clarkson had got through to the post office. He put his hand over the receiver.

"Miss Ash, we don't want to cause a lot of talk, would you say that you had intended to post a book before lunch for Mrs. Robson, but find that you must have left it behind you at The Clearing. Did Mrs. Robson post it herself?"

Margaret did as asked. She was told that Mrs. Robson had not been into the post office today.

Clarkson held out a scrap of paper in front of her. She read from it into the receiver.

"Perhaps someone else posted it? Has any book, too thick to go into the pillar box, been handed in this morning?"

"No book of any kind, thick or thin, has been handed over the counter. The postwoman's just in for the next collection. If it's important I'll ask her if she found any books in the before-noon collection today," volunteered the postmistress.

"Oh do," said Margaret in reply to Findlay and Clarkson's energetic nods.

The reply came that the postwoman had not found any books in any collection she had made that day, including the one just taken up.

"Did you see what Mrs. Robson wrote on the flyleaf?" asked the constable.

"Yes. It was *In memory of Posey* and it was dated for tomorrow."

Margaret now continued to look around the room for any changes. Suddenly she bent forward.

"This wasn't here when I left. What is it?" She held up the short length of chain with the padlock on one end they had all examined. "I've never seen this before."

"Mr. Robson thinks his wife got it ready for the new dog when she telephoned for him to your place," said Clarkson.

Margaret dropped it.

"She must have meant to be sure he wouldn't run away," she said a trifle dryly.

"Now about the leather coat Mrs. Robson used to wear," Findlay went on, "we found one burning in the stove, and want, of course, to find out to whom it belonged."

"Well, it couldn't have been the one Zilla threw away. Annabelle must have bought another." She looked inquiringly at Robson, who said that he knew nothing about a new coat.

"Would you recognize the buttons on the coat she gave your sister?" Clarkson asked next.

"No, I'm sure I couldn't," said Margaret, who was very pale.

"I thought you had seen it very often on Mrs. Robson"

"Yes, but only from a distance. And I never saw my sister wearing it."

"Still—as a guess, what color would you say that the buttons were?" Clarkson pressed.

"Ivory yellow, I seem to recollect," said Margaret

"Is this a button from the coat?" asked Clarkson, holding out the button which Tyrwhitt had found.

"Looks like it," said Margaret, turning it over and over. "Yes," she said as she handed it back, "this looks like one of them."

"Now, when was the last time that your sister wore Mrs. Robson's coat? As near as you can remember? Please think carefully."

She thought a moment. Her face was white not merely pale.

"About a month ago."

They all saw that she was under some great strain. Findlay motioned to Clarkson to take her upstairs while he stepped to the telephone, and rang up Mrs. Ash.

It was another voice, a full, rather husky voice that answered.

"Zilla Ash speaking," it said.

Findlay asked her if she would come to the police station at once, and there be kind enough to answer a few questions about the late Mrs. Robson.

"You want to see *me*? How thrilling! What for?"

"We are questioning everyone who knew Mrs. Robson. And you, as a friend, may well have a fresh angle on her character."

"I'll be there on my bike in ten minutes."

He waited five minutes then he rang again. This time it was Mrs. Ash who came to the instrument.

"Mrs. Ash, we're interested in that leather coat of Mrs. Robson's which she passed on to Miss Ash. Do you remember it?"

"I do. Mrs. Robson gave it to my elder daughter for her farming work," came the reply after a second, "but I haven't seen her wearing it for some time."

"Would you look and see if it's in her wardrobe?"

There followed a little wait, then the voice told him that Mrs. Ash could not see it anywhere.

Findlay hung up. He did not like the look of things at all.

When Margaret and Clarkson came downstairs, Findlay asked her a few more questions about the dead woman's social circle, of which the girl knew nothing, and then asked her if she would be good enough to make her way to the police station and make a formal deposition of what she had just told them.

That done, he sat down to make his own notes of the case. Tyrwhitt stood by the window smoking, and mentally trying to arrange the facts so far known in some sort of order.

Robson sat in a chair, his head in his hands.

At that moment, a car could be heard drawing up outside the gate. Robson went to the window.

Two men came towards the house.

"Whitehouse and Green," said Robson, as they came in sight.

The author was walking in front. He was a man of early middle age, with dark brown hair parted in the middle, a noble brow, big but dreamy eyes, a kindly but weak mouth, and a still weaker chin. As for his secretary, Green was a big man with a lean, hatchet face of the predatory type, and long, strong looking hands. Whitehouse either was always very pale, or was so now.

"'We've heard the dreadful news," he said breathlessly, in a pleasant rich voice to Robson as he came up to the Window.

"Dreadful!" repeated Green, stepping inside.

"I can't grasp it yet," was Robson's reply. "All this seems like something I'm seeing on the films—not a real thing at all. This is the chief constable, Major Findlay."

The major introduced his nephew, then he left them talking and strolled to the gate. There he had a swift look at the Lagonda outside. At the back, on the floor, under a rug, was a railway time table with a big red ink stain on its paper cover. It certainly looked like the missing A.B.C. Findlay left the book where it was, and joined the group in the house. He asked Robson and Green to wait upstairs while the police talked to Whitehouse.

"Would you begin by telling us all you know of Mrs. Robson?" he suggested, taking a seat himself.

"I've dandled her on my knees many a time when she was yelling the roof off," said Whitehouse with a reminiscent smile. "Perhaps I'd better explain about myself first. My father, Henry Whitehouse, was Lord Shipley's third son. He developed lung trouble after Eton and a year at Cambridge. So he went off to Austalia. After, a few changes, he drifted to the farm of a man named William Eighteen. He had two daughters. My father promptly fell in love with one and married her. The other daughter was already married to a rancher called Bigger, who lived up country. My father bought a ranch nearby, and they lived there very happily. My mother died when I was born. My father nearly went mad. He hated the sight of me, and things got so bad that one of his hands wrote to my aunt, Nellie Bigger, who came in person and took me off with her to her own home. No boy could have had a happier home than my aunt and her husband made for me. She had a child—Annabelle— the only child she ever had—the year after I got there, and, as I say, many a time I've dandled that squalling kid on these knees.

"Later, when my father died, I inherited a thousand pounds, which was to be spent, or partly spent, in sending me to Cambridge. I came home, was sent by my people to a good coach, and got a scholarship for Trinity. That settled my life, more or less. I wrote for the *Granta*. My father's father seemed to be interested in me at long last, and, with his help, I took a first in Law, then proceeded to eat my dinners, and finally became a member of the Middle Temple. I started writing while waiting for briefs, and found the work so much to my taste that I turned writer in earnest. Green was sent to me by an agency, to whom I applied for a good secretary, some four years ago, and has been with me ever since.

"Now to come to Robson. His father was a well-known expert in plant diseases—plant doctor as he himself, and the Biggers' nearest neighbor. Robson was working most of the time, but we used to meet when we could. In due course, he and Annabelle got engaged, and were married in—let me see—years ago it was. They came over to England because times were very bad over in Australia just then for anyone connected with land. Annabelle had a few hundreds that came to her from a grandmother and they put it into buying this place after one in South Wales. I had quite lost sight of Annabelle and of Robson, when I got a letter from Mrs. Bigger a year ago, asking me to look up Annabelle. Aunt Nell was worried about her daughter. Her letters were so short and dull that she was afraid her daughter wasn't happy. Mind you, Aunt Nell was devoted to her son-in-law, Harold Robson, and she was a very good judge of a man too, she was worried because something—we know that it was overwork and bitter poverty—made the daughter's letters far apart and very short. Annabelle was game, you see, and, knowing how hard hit her parents were, too, by things out there, always wrote as though, financially, she and Robson were doing fairly well. But Aunt Nell wrote me to say that the years of drought had broken at long last, and she enclosed fifty pounds for her along with Annabelle's address. Her idea—or Uncle Bill's idea really—was for me to have a look for myself and a talk with Annabelle before handing over the money. If things were going well between husband and wife, I was to tell them that the fifty was to be followed by a regular pound a week. That meant that the Robsons would have what would virtually come to two pounds a week for the first year. So I came along to Lincolnshire. Found it more beautiful than I had imagined, with air that sets you up like wine—or at least it does me—and found also a quite exhausted husband

and wife, but devoted to each other. There was no doubt of that."

"Just how did you meet them?" Tyrwhitt asked.

"Met him in the first place at the gate of The Clearing, and we had a talk of old times. I had gone out to see them both, but the poor chap had found Annabelle lying in a dead faint on the kitchen floor the day before and had to put her to bed. But when I did meet her, I didn't need to wonder whether to hand over the money or not, I never saw a couple more in love with one another than those two. And that's the local verdict, I may tell you."

Superintendent Clarkson nodded a vigorous assent.

"Well, that money made all the difference to them both. Robson at once got a woman to come in daily, and a boy who was to do Annabelle's work in the holding, so that, with the double help, she was soon blooming like a rose again."

"I stayed a couple of days with them, but—well, two is company, believe me, so I pushed on to Tealby, where I took the Manor house furnished. Next came a telephone call from an excited Annabelle. A distant Eighteen had died leaving everything to his next of kin, who, as my mother was dead, was only Aunt Nell. Aunt Nell had inherited something that amounted to a little under a million English pounds, after paying death duties. She wanted Annabelle and Robson to go home to her. Before they could, she was run over and killed. Aunt Nell's will—" here Whitehouse repeated what the police already knew about the will, and Bigger's hopeless illness.

Mr. Whitehouse leaned back in his chair. The room was getting filled with the rich, herby smell of good, juniper. Mr. Whitehouse must have had a stiff drink or two before coming to The Clearing. Similar waves had spread themselves whenever Green opened his mouth.

"Now, a very important question, Mr. Whitehouse. Are you absolutely certain of the identity of the Robsons. Especially of Mrs. Robson?"

Whitehouse stared a moment, and then burst into amused laughter.

"Absolutely! Apart from recognizing them, if you had heard them swapping old recollections with me you wouldn't ask that question. Mrs. Robson would talk for hours about the old days she spent out there."

"It's because of the face being destroyed that we have to make sure of there being no mistake," Findlay explained.

"That looks more like a woman's doing than a man's," murmured Whitehouse.

"Was Mrs. Robson an aggravating type?" asked Tyrwhitt.

"Not when I first met her again," Whitehouse said after a second's pause "But, little by little, her wealth changed her more than I would have believed possible."

They waited for him to explain.

"From a warm-hearted affectionate little thing, devoted to her husband, her old home, and her parents— well, she changed."

"Into what?" asked Findlay.

"Only keen on having a good time."

"But she was still in love with her husband?" asked Clarkson.

Whitehouse gave the equivalent of a shrug.

"As far as I know, yes, but she changed so much in every other way. The money went to her head."

"And Robson? Did it change him?"

"Harold?" said Whitehouse "Steady going chaps like him don't change."

"You think he was as much in love with his wife as ever?"

"Just as much."

"What about Mrs. Robson having a love affair —a quite recent one unknown to her husband?" asked Findlay.

"I wouldn't be surprised at anything," was the reply.

"Has Robson a violent temper, would you say?"

"Yes," was the reply. "At least he had as a boy. Smouldering underground, and then bursting out into flames when the last straw was added."

"Now about your tenancy of this house. Do you mind explaining how you came to take it over?"

"When Mrs. Robson came into that money on Aunt Nell's death, she naturally decided that she could do better than stay on here. She wanted to sell this little cottage, but Robson refused. Said they had both put too much heartache and backache into The Clearing ever to sell it. Well, I was beginning to get tired of the house at Tealby, and it was agreed that the place would be handed over to me on a quarterly rent."

Whitehouse poured himself out a very stiff gin and lime juice, after pressing the others to have some.

"And now about today?" Findlay asked. Whitehouse put down his tumbler with reluctance.

"Better have Green in. I never get times, or dates, right."

Green was sent for.

Whitehouse, promptly, poured himself out another drink. He nodded toward his secretary.

"Go ahead," he said briefly.

Green said that Whitehouse and he motored into Lincoln for a book wanted by Whitehouse. That, as usual, they had roamed around the old town, looking at some old prints, and books, and after buying the book in question, had turned into one of the cinemas and seen "My German Wife;" a rattling spy film and then, after another leisurely amble through the streets and a couple of drinks at the Saracen's Head and tea at the White Hart had driven home, to be told the terrible news by a postman who had passed them a little distance down the road.

"You realize, of course, gentlemen, that we must check up all this," said Findlay. He scribbled quickly on his writing pad.

"I'll go in by train myself," volunteered Clarkson.

"Have you an A.B.C.?" he asked suddenly.

"In the car," and Green rose, to return a minute or so later with the stained copy which Findlay had already seen.

Clarkson took it, made as though to open it at the L's, and then seemed to see the red ink for the first time.

"But this—why, this is the A.B.C. seen in the sitting room just before lunch!" He spoke sharply. "It was described to us, and we have all been hunting for it. How do you account for its being in your car?"

Whitehouse gripped the table. His face went a green-white. His lips were gray.

"This time-table was not in this house this morning," came Green's voice sharply. "I ought to know, I took it back to the inn with me last night when we dropped in here as usual, for coffee after dinner. There's some mistake—or a try-on," he finished on an ugly note.

The color flooded back to Whitehouse's face. So much so, that now it was red as it had been white.

Findlay knew better than to force the issue. It would be two person's word against that of the pair here—nothing but a stalemate. He asked instead if Mr. Whitehouse would be kind enough to drive, or himself be driven, to the police station, and there dictate and sign his statement of the day's doings.

"While I want Mr. Green to stay here, go over the cottage, and see if things are exactly as always—or whether anything has been shifted, taken away or added to."

Whitehouse looked hard at Green, who looked back at him with an easy, encouraging smile.

"Why not?" he asked; and added to the superintendent: "Mr. Whitehouse is one of those chaps who don't like the police. Wrong nursery training. While I was brought up to always turn to a bobby in time of trouble."

Findlay drew his nephew on one side.

"You do as you like about staying. I'm going to take Whitehouse on to the police station, after which I must be off home. See you and Clarkson at dinner." And with a nod, the major passed on.

Clarkson and Green could be heard tramping about overhead. Tyrwhitt lit a cigarette from a box on the mantel and tried to think over what they had just heard.

A crunch on the gravel made him go to the window. A moment later a thin, short man came into view. The newcomer stopped almost in front of Tyrwhitt and stared at the little house, his eyes slowly traveling over it, almost brick by brick, it seemed to the Army man. Then he heard him come into the house by the front door, and after a word with the constable in the passage, come on into the room

He acted as though Tyrwhitt were invisible. Choosing a chair, he placed it against the wall and sat down on it, his eyes closed, his head tilted back. The man was breathing deeply, very slowly and very regularly.

In a few minutes Clarkson and Green came back again.

"Nothing changed, Mr. Green thinks," said the superintendent, "except, of course, the position of the rifle and the fact that two shots have been fired from it."

"Hello, Acland! I wondered when you'd turn up. This is Mr. Acland, sir," he turned to Tyrwhitt, "our organist and local reporter."

At last the newcomer looked at Captain Tyrwhitt with a pair of very light gray eyes. The lashes and eyebrows were so fair that they appeared non-existent. Apparently the only hair on his face was a long, fluttering reddish mustache that spread out at the ends over a small, mean looking, effeminate mouth.

"How d'y do," grunted Acland. "Yes, I've come on behalf of the paper, of course."

"Did you know Mrs. Robson?" Tyrwhitt asked.

"Oh, quite well." Acland did not lower his nasal ones. "Quite well. I was right, you see, Superintendent," Acland now addressed Clarkson, "about a tragedy in this house, I mean. That's why I tried, to get into the house. I could have warned her, but I ever had the chance."

"You said it was a past tragedy you felt," replied Clarkson in the tone of a man pouncing on a glaring overclaim.

Acland shrugged.

"One can never tell past from present or future in such impressions. There is no time in the spirit world. But I wasn't out about its being a murder, was I?"

Clarkson gave him a measuring look.

"No, Mr. Acland, you were right about that. Funny."

"Funny—peculiar, eh? Why so? When I helped you over those stolen library books, you didn't think funny. But now, about this murder, what's the story for the press?"

Clarkson told it briefly, and then indicated Green, with a sort of gesture that suggested that Acland could get what he liked from him.

"Let's see, your boss comes into all the rest of that Australian fortune, doesn't he?" said Acland casually.

"Ask him, don't ask me," said Green.

"And if Robson had been killed, *everything* would have come to him, eh?"

"You seem better informed about it all than I am," said Green rudely.

"I wouldn't say that," in a detached, ironic voice and with a glitter of light eyes, "but naturally as the local newspaper man, I had to look up the question of Mrs. Robson's sudden good fortune thoroughly. As thoroughly as you did," he carelessly. Then he put his pen back, and looked at Clarkson again.

"You've something in your pocket that belongs to this case. Can I have a word with you in private?"

Clarkson suggested that Mr. Green would be good as to walk down to the police station to have his deposition taken down.

Green agreed after a little grumbling. When he was out of the gate, Clarkson turned to Tyrwhitt.

"I ought to explain to you that Mr Acland claims to have some sort of second sight."

"Sort of!" repeated Acland sarcastically. "You have something that belongs to the case. Something small—in your coat pocket," he repeated.

"That would be a very likely guess," Tyrwhitt thought.

Clarkson drew out a paper envelope, folded it in his handkerchief, and held it out.

"See what you can make of that Mr. Acland. By second sight."

"Second nothing!" retored Acland. "My dear chap, this is psychometry—as much second sight about it as about your radio. You ought to be able to do it yourself. A hundred years from now every policeman will have to pass a test in it. But I'll see what I can pick up about whatever it is you've handed me."

He sat down again on the chair and leaned his head back, one hand holding the handkerchief, the other lightly resting on it.

"Blood—blood, blood -blood everywhere," said Acland in his high voice.

Clarkson looked at Tyrwhitt and shook his head. There had not been blood everywhere.

"Two women!" said Acland suddenly and sharply "I see two women distinctly in it." He frowned, and after a moment, almost flung the handkerchief to Clarkson.

"It's no good. That's all I get. I'm not receptive enough. The thing's too near me. I begin to wonder who the other woman is—and what it means that's fatal."

"But you think another woman's in it. Not a man?" Clarkson asked slowly.

"Can't say about a man as well. All I got was a certainty of two women being concerned, and that whatever you handed me had been concerned in the murder, steeped in blood. Well," he rose, "sorry I couldn't see further this time, but I must be off and get the tale ready for the press. Remember—two women!" and with that he nodded casually and rose to leave them, but the door was pushed open from the other side and Robson strode in. He turned sharply at the sight of the little man close to the door.

"Do you mind staying on the other side of the gate? Mr. Whitehouse made us promise not to let you in. My wife complained to me yesterday about your trying to scrape up an acquaintance with her."

"I felt there was something evil in this cottage, and I tried to get a clearer impression of what it was," said Acland, making no move "If your wife complained of me, she was under a misapprehension—so is Whitehouse."

"The only impression I want you to get clear is that if I catch you on this side of the gate, you'll be distinctly, sorry for it."

"Threats, eh?" asked Acland with an unpleasant smile.

"Threats," Robson assented "From my tenant as well as from myself. If you think that anyone she objected to is going to strut about her home; well—just try it!"

"Mrs. Robson had no more cause to object to me than has Whitehouse—"

"Possibly—and possibly not! But—remember—the other side of the gate is the side for you. Anything you want to know, you can find out from the police, or by telephone."

"No offense meant," Acland muttered.

Robson watched him go, and stamped down the path after him. A moment later, they heard a gate shut with a bang that suggested Robson's handd rather than Acland's.

Tyrwhitt and Clarkson exchanged grins. "Couldn't interfere with a man warning another off his premises," said the superintendent, "especially he made no definite threats."

Robson returned on that.

"Whitehouse was very definite about him. He caught him roaming around one day. My wife and I had to promise him not to let the chap in. However, I don't think he'll stay about much now. Perhaps it's a pity I spoke as I did. After all, they say he's a good reporter." His voice sounded weary. "Certainly this case will need all the help it can get."

The superintendent was putting his papers together.

"I shall want to look over Mrs. Robson's personal belongings at Windhill tomorrow," said Clarkson.

"I'll lock the door of her room as soon as I get things out of it, and hand you over the key," and with that Robson hurried off towards the corner, from which a bus would take him past the police station, where he promised to call in and make his statement.

"What's this about Acland and that button?" asked Tyrwhitt after a moment "It was the button from the coat that you handed him, I saw."

"He's a queer bloke," said Clarkson. "Helped us once very much when it was a question of some thefts of books from the village library. Helped us so much that, between ourselves, we have kept an eye on him ever since. The next time I tried him was a complete washout. All wrong all along the line. As he was today. Two women may be right, or wrong, but 'steeped in blood' the coat couldn't have been. Two women, eh? Well we shall see. But if Acland's rung the bell this time again, we shall do more than just keep our eyes on him," he added, under breath. "We made some inquiries when he knew so much about the place where the stolen books were found, and learned that he wasn't considered a satisfactory citizen in his last home. Nothing definite, but he kept queer company. He's a rum bird, is Acland."

CHAPTER FOUR

After dinner in the chief constable's house that evening, the talk turned on the murder at The Clearing.

"The alibis of Whitehouse and Green are absolutely impossible to check up on, but one, or both, must have been back to the house after the younger Ash girl left. If she's telling the truth about that train book," said Clarkson.

"I thought she was," said Tyrwhitt.

"It's a lot to say," said his uncle a little grimly; "but I'm sure of it. And she'll make a good impression on any jury."

"Her local reputation makes me sure of it, sir. In the last blitz she did wonders, silently, quietly. I think we can take what she says as absolutely true."

"I could imagine that striking looking sister of hers doing good work in a blitz too," said Findlay, "yet I wouldn't believe a word she said. I thought she was going to fling things at us when we pressed her about the coat." He turned to Tyrwhitt; "Her story is that it was old when it was given to her, that it soon got past use, and that she thrust the tattered bits into one of the salvage bins of the village. Nearly two months ago she thinks. As the tins are emptied by the local dustmen weekly, it's not likely that it was noticed—even if there."

"She says that she put no name or distinguishing mark whatever on it. And there Miss Margaret bears her out," said Clarkson.

"I noticed she didn't agree that it was past use, or in any, such state as to justify throwing it into the refuse bins," Findlay helped himself to another cup of coffee, "but then, I should fancy that where clothing was concerned, Miss Ash would be a trifle particular."

"Just a trifle, sir," agreed Clarkson grinning. "By the way," Clarkson turned to Tyrwhitt, "Whitehouse definitely identifies that button as belonging to Mrs. Robson's leather coat. The coat was a wedding present from her mother and father. Specially selected and treated skins, and the buttons are made only in Canberra, from local, horn set in local wood. Annabelle Robson showed him the coat on one of his first visits, and said how fond she was of it.

"I never saw Mrs. Robson in anything else in the early days after they came down here. In fact, until Mr. Whitehouse appeared on the scene with help from Canberra, it was her uniform. Just a white ghost stooping and bending, weeding and digging on her allotment from dawn to dusk. Gosh, how that woman worked!" Clarkson was thinking of some of his constables.

"I can't quite make out why the coat was burned, with all the stink it was bound to make. Sounds the silly thing a woman might do who lost her head, of course." Tyrwhitt was very perplexed "Any stains could have been washed off—any cuts or tears put down to some other cause—"

"Yes, and it must have taken longer to souse in paraffin and stuff it into the stove than it would have done to wipe it," mused his uncle aloud, "even though no attempt was made—apparently—to hide the fact that the coat was being burned. It's a most extraordinary case," the chief constable continued, "the Case of the Inconclusive Clues would be its best name."

"How do you mean?" asked Tyrwhitt

"Well, take the case of a husband who tells his wife he won't be home till the next day and then gets back by lunch time. Typical jealous, or at least suspicious, husband act. But we can hear of no jealousy." He looked inquiringly at Clarkson who shook his head.

"Not a hint of it, sir. Though, mind you, everyone agrees, I do myself, in thinking that Mrs. Robson's money changed her a bit—and not for the better. But Robson hasn't changed, And by Jove, sir," he said suddenly, "he

would have had to change to kill the goose that was due
to lay an egg of that size—two-thirds of a million pounds.
Mrs. Robson, and Whitehouse, both had a cable this
morning saying that Mr. Bigger is sinking fast, and that
the end is expected any hour. The cable was in Mrs.
Robson's handbag. Robson says she showed it to him
before he left for Gainsborough."

"And she seems to have been entirely indifferent to
her father's illness. Affectionate daughter." The major
spoke dryly.

"I know, sir. Mr. Whitehouse says that each time he
has seen her since the money came to her she has shown
more and more elation at her changed circumstances and
grown steadily more completely indifferent to her old
home"

"That's natural, I'm afraid, to some characters,"
Clarkson thought, and the others agreed

"To begin at the beginning—why did Mrs. Robson
send for the dog—what's your explanation of that?"
Findlay turned to his nephew.

"Heard noises in the house," Tyrwhitt guessed
promptly

"Then why not ask a man to bring the dog over? Why
only ask for Margaret Ash?"

"Thought she heard rats," was Tyrwhitt's belief, "and
wanted the dog, but felt no need of help."

"Was it Annabelle Robson who telephoned?"

"I think it must have been," Clarkson put in "I can't
see why the murderer should summon witnesses."

"Curious that the dog which was sent for was the
same dog who was killed," mused the chief constable.
"That request for the dog—well, it's odd, to my mind. But,
on the whole, I think, like you, Superintendent, that it
must have been the deceased who rang up the Ashes, but
then, what made her voice sound so queer, as Mrs. Ash
insists that it did?"

"And this coat," Clarkson continued the list. "What on
earth was it burned for?"

"Just so, Clarkson. Burned coat points clearly to an effort to get rid of incriminating stains—and so, in this case, turns out to be no signpost at all."

"Like the smashed face—pointing to substitution. Therefore, in this case standing for something quite different. I suppose we shall find next that the dog was wanted for something quite different from anything so far guessed."

"Of course the man who stands to profit enormously is Whitehouse. Against its being him, however," said Tyrwhitt, "is that he's not a fool. Supposing him to have been the murderer, he's been amazingly stupid. To murder her here at The Clearing, and not to provide himself with a good alibi."

"Not so easy," said his uncle. "You try it—mentally, of course! Commit a crime at four o'clock say, how are you going to have it look as though you were somewhere else? Whitehouse's alibi—supposing it to be concocted, as we do, isn't so bad. While Green swears they were together in Lincoln, there's always a chance we can't prove they weren't."

"I've just been wondering . . ." Clarkson said after a long silence. "If Robson's story is true, whoever did the killing probably expected to have till the next day to tidy up. I've been wondering whether that bashed in face might not have been the first step to misleading us as to who had been killed. Say Mrs. Robson's body was to have been carried away to some other place, and left somewhere on the road in the blackout to look like an accident."

"That's possible," said the chief constable after reflecting a moment, "in which case the murderer—if it was Whitehouse, say—might have intended to stage a very well worked out mystery. One with no clue as to the identity of the murdered woman—"

"And something would, of course, have been done to keep the husband from suspecting that it was his wife who was dead. Say he had a letter from her speaking of a visit to some friends—or some place."

"And that might be why the top sheet of the blotter was missing. The murderer might have had to make more than one attempt to imitate her writing."

"Yes, that might explain the blotting paper having been taken away—or more probably burnt in the stove," agreed Findlay.

"I think it might even explain the missing book," Clarkson was thinking aloud "Suppose Mrs. Robson asked the murderer to send it off for her, since Miss Ash had forgotten it, and he slipped it into his pocket. Well, after the murder and the attempted murder of Robson, he would have to get rid of it. Which would be easily done."

"You think Robson interrupted a possible masterpiece?" queried Tyrwhitt. "No wonder whoever it was tried to shoot him. But I still don't see where the burnt coat fits in. Nor that torn-off button. It would have taken a very strong pull to tear that coat, and I think we're agreed that the room showed no sign of a tussle."

"The money?" asked Clarkson. "The missing sixty pounds?"

Major Findlay nodded. "Looks like it. Can't think of any other reason to squabble over the coat. And the money is missing, we're told. And Robson still maintains that the missing sixty one pound notes were the reason for the murder."

"Possibly they are missing just to give that idea," Clarkson maintained "Also, isn't it possible that the murderer thought they might come in handy if things went wrong, and he had to make a getaway? Besides, if it's Whitehouse, then Green is in it—after, if not before, and will need money to keep him compliant."

"Miss Ash gave a very curious performance when she was questioned at the station," Clarkson looked, at Findlay as though for permission to continue "She knows more than she said, I think."

"Holding something back, but whether a lot, or a little, I couldn't be certain. You take a dramatic performer like Miss Zilla Ash, and a little might easily seem to them a lot if it touched themselves." Tyrwhitt was gazing into his glass as into a crystal.

"Would it surprise you to know that I overheard this same Ash girl yesterday morning making violent love to Robson in the woods? And he telling her not to be a fool?"

"Miss Ash?" asked Clarkson in profound surprise, "why she's to marry young Mr. Bramwell next month!"

"Well, she was taking Robson in her stride then, or trying to."

"Can you repeat the talk?" asked his uncle.

"I don't know if I can give the actual words, but they ran along these lines: I was strolling aimlessly about, when I became aware of a woman's voice not far away. It grew louder, and I heard it say, 'I can't believe you! Damn it all; what can you see in that little fool?' Man's voice replies, 'Do you mind not talking of my wife like that? I happen to be in love with her'. 'Rats!' said the lady, or a word to that effect, 'You're talking through your hat! She bores you as she does me.' Then there was a sort of rustling sound. I think she had thrown her arms around him and he was sidestepping them. I peeped through a couple of bushes, and saw the girl pointed out to me as Zilla Ash, facing a man with his back to me. 'For God's sake,'—I think these were his actual words—'for God's sake leave me alone. I can't stand any more of this persecution. I love my wife, I don't love you, and never shall. Will nothing get that into your head? You call Annabelle a fool, it's you who are the fool.' With that—" Tyrwhitt's teeth showed white, "she stepped back a pace, and next came an almighty smack on his tanned and manly face. She whirled, and was gone. Robson stood a second swearing under his breath. Then he, too, stamped away—in the opposite direction to that the lady had taken."

"Well—well—well!" murmured Findlay with a chuckle.

"Mrs. Rogers might know something," Clarkson said slowly, "she's the postmistress we talked to about the book; and what she doesn't know about all of us—" he left the sentence unfinished

"I can imagine that Miss Ash, wearing the leather coat, might have looked in at The Clearing this morning. Say she found Mrs. Robson dead. Isn't it possible that it was she who battered her dead rival's face—from rage— jealous rage? Marked the coat in doing so, and had to burn it, as she daren't have it found bloodstained. I think that might account for two bits of the puzzle, the face and the burnt coat. . ."

"But the murderer was still in the house, according to Robson's story of what happened afterwards—the shots at himself," his uncle reminded him.

"I don't suppose Miss Ash was long. Three minutes would do it all. Say the murderer slipped upstairs when he heard her come in, he would still be upstairs waiting for Robson when she left, and Robson would get there a few minutes after she gone."

"It could have happened like that," said Findlay, "though it makes the Ash girl out to be a horrible creature."

"She seems to be an odd mixture, sir," said Clarkson. "Nothing known against her in our line, except speeding, of course. She's a good, but very reckless driver. Also, she's said to be an uncommonly hard worker, and that's not what you would expect from her appearance. Swears like a trooper, can drink a man under the table at the pubs they say, but never late on her job. And what she says she'll do and where she says she'll go, she does—and goes in spite of ice, snow and blinding hail, broken back axle, or what-not."

"She's liked?"

"Very popular with the women. Not so much with the men. I take it she won't put up with slack work. She's a funny mixture. Where her promises are connected with her work, they say you can depend on her absolutely, but otherwise, she's the reputation of being absolutely unreliable and absolutely unscrupulous. Says anything. Promises anything to get what she wants, or get out of what she doesn't want. Owes every shop in the village. They say Brownlow, the jeweler, is getting worried about her bill."

"Umph," said Major Findlay. "Money difficulties . . . Wild—resolute—self-willed—not too good, after what Captain Tyrwhitt saw, or rather heard. No, not too good. . ."

"There aren't many suspects so far," said the chief constable. "We agree that usually the husband, no matter how devoted he may seem, has the place of honor. And Robson could—just barely— have been the murderer here. Say he didn't drive slowly when passing Uthwatt, but let the car out. He could have dashed up to the gate, rushed to the house, caught sight of his wife and a lover, banged her over the head, during which the man decamps, and then killed the dog, fired through his own hat, crammed the coat into the stove, and rushed into the road shouting his wife's name and calling on someone to stop!"

"Why bring along a dog for which he had just paid fifty pounds, in order to shoot him? It would have had to be dashed quick work, sir," said Clarkson.

"Is he of a jealous nature?" asked Tyrwhitt.

"Never had the need to be," said Clarkson, "as far as any of us in the village know. But from what I've seen of him, I should say quite definitely that he's not the jealous type. Very fond of his wife and all that, but I can't imagine him getting into a fury over anything she did. Besides, sir, as I say, I don't think Mrs. Robson had eyes for anyone but her husband, but supposing she had, would she have invited one of the Ash girls to come along?"

"Ah!" said Findlay, "that's the insuperable objection in my mind to any theory of a lover this afternoon with Mrs. Robson. That message proves, I think, that there could have been no scene to meet the returned husband's eyes which would turn him into an instant murderer. That being so, quite apart from the time difficulty, I think one can hardly understand why, even supposing he wanted to get rid of his wife, he would not have put things off for a day or so, knowing Mr. Bigger was dying."

"You bet Robson would, sir!" said Clarkson instantly.

"No," continued the major, "I think, for once, that the husband is here out of the direct line of suspects. That leaves, of those we know so far, only Whitehouse and Green, with, possibly, Miss, Ash as some sort of an accessory."

"One of the men could have got hold of the coat when it was thrown out—if it was thrown out," said Tyrwhitt, "and used it—as an apron."

"If Miss Ash had worn it she would surely have taken good care to have had it thoroughly destroyed," said Clarkson.

"No time," Findlay pointed out. "Whoever the criminal was, he had to work at lightning speed. Which is why that destroyed face must mean that it was one step in a job he hadn't time to finish. The same holds good of the half-burned coat. Miss Ash looked to me pretty hot stuff if she really got worked up."

"I wonder if Acland could have seen her going or coming from The Clearing," speculated Clarkson.

"Apparently he has been hanging around The Clearing quite a bit, according to Green. Whitehouse found him a frightful bore, and had an idea he was interested in his papers, and told him to keep away. It seems that Whitehouse is getting out a book on ballistics for the W.O. If Acland saw her, he may have seen a good deal more," said Findlay. "I don't like that chap. We'll see what his paper has to say about the murder tomorrow morning. He may show some unauthorized knowledge."

"Any watch being kept on the suspects?" asked Tyrwhitt.

"Not enough men," was the superintendent's reply. "I've notified the railway stations, and all police, of course, and the bus services are warned to keep their eyes open, in case any of our friends think of roaming a bit far from home. I shall keep an eye on the White Hind myself. Mrs. Brownlow is letting me have a shakedown in a cupboard which either Whitehouse or Green must pass, if they stir out of their rooms."

"Shall I have one of your police cars watch by the gates?" asked Tyrwhitt.

"Wouldn't be a bad idea," agreed Clarkson. "If you see their gray Lagonda go after her. Not that I think they can give me the slip, but it's better to be on the safe side."

"Right I won't show up in the White Hind at all, but will be on hand, with lights out, drawn up close under the shelter of a hedge."

The telephone rang.

"Who is speaking, please? Oh, Miss Ash? You want to offer Mr. Robson a room at Ing's Place for the night, as he may not have any place to go? That's very kind of you, but Mr. Robson isn't here. He's at the railway station possibly. Or more probably in the Lincoln train. But he expects to be back in the morning, and if you like to telephone to him then . . ." He hung up.

"Persistent gel!" said Tyrwhitt appreciatively.

At the other end, Zilla, very pale, and with some thing tense in face and carriage which none of her family had ever seen before, dropped the receiver hastily and made for the door.

"I'm off for the night," she called to her mother in the sitting room "On duty, Promised to help Catherine with her night work. See you in the morning," and with that she was gone, running down the drive and out of the gates and across a short cut to the railway station. She just made it and scrambled into the train as the flag was being waved. At Grantham she got out quickly, waited by the train till she saw Robson pass, and hurried after him. When both were through the barrier, she touched him on the arm.

He gave her a look of exasperation.

"I must have a word with you," she said.

"Get in." It was his turn to issue commands, as he motioned to a railway taxi. She settled herself gracefully in the corner of cab.

"Now then!" He turned to face her.

"Oh dear no," was the composed reply, "not in the taxi."

"Where do you suggest then?"

"Suppose we get out, and walk through the gardens here. Tell the taxi to take your things on to your house."

He agreed to this, and they turned together through the wooden gates that replaced the iron ones of before the war.

"'What do you want to talk to me about?" Robson asked, as he followed her.

She only flashed her great eyes at him and turned down a footpath. There she leaned over an empty bench and stared straight ahead of her, yet with something in her attitude that suggested that she was listening intently to her companion, to his very breathing, one would have said.

"What's the matter with you, Zilla?" he said in a low, fierce tone, after a full minute's silence.

"What do you think is the matter with me?" she asked, facing him now. "I didn't spoil your fairy tale to the police, just now, did I?" she asked with a sneer, but her eyes were hot. "I heard every word through the door into the room where we were all sitting."

"What?" The word came with the effect of shot.

She hushed him with a raised finger. It was a theatrical little gesture of hers which intensely irritated her family.

"What the devil do you think you're saying?" he asked, in a lowered tone. "You—ho—who—" He shut his teeth for a second, and then said in a ton of horror, "You, who stamped her face into the mud. Why did you do that to her face?"

"You can save your breath," she replied shortly "I happened to have been just outside The Clearing when that rifle was fired. I saw you fire it."

For a second the glare in his eyes silenced her.

"It's no use trying to deny it," she repeated. "I saw you at your bedroom window—the rifle in your hand—"

"Liar!" was the reply, in a voice of deepest horror.

"I saw you. I saw you. I saw you," she almost screamed the words in his ear. "I saw you at the window—"

"Listen, you fool!" he said hoarsely. "I was laying flattened out on the gravel path. If you're telling the truth, who did you see? Who?"

"You!" she repeated angrily. "Think I don't know you, Harold Robson?"

"Get, this straight. You didn't see me, for I didn't murder Annabelle. You saw her murderer, if you're not telling some invention." He bent forward and stared into her eyes "You couldn't have seen his face or you would know it wasn't me. My God, why didn't you—" then he broke off.

"Exactly!" she replied, an angry light in her eyes. "Why didn't I tell the police?"

"But the face," he persisted, his voice shaking. "Don't play with me, Zilla, you, and you alone, may be able to help us find the man. What was his face like? He must have looked like me—but—did you see him clearly?"

For the first-time she looked uncertain.

"I—I—I thought it was you," she whispered.

"The face, girl!" he begged "What was his face like?"

"His head was turned sideways, putting the gun back carefully, very carefully by the window. But the coat—the tie—the hair—he wore your hat. I do remember now that he wore it a lot lower than you do—pulled over his forehead. Harold"—she was looking wildly at him—"then what you told to the police was what really happened?"

"What really happened," he said between his teeth. "But that crushed face—your coat in the scullery stove—oh, if I knew which way truth lies. Where were you?"

He got her story out of her piecemeal. She said that she had hung about The Clearing hoping to see him, not knowing that he had gone to Gainsborough early that morning. Then she had gone off and mended some of her egg baskets. That done, about noon, she had returned to The Clearing, thinking he would be back for lunch, and climbed into an old oak tree. Later she had heard two shots fired—and staring at the window from which smoke was coming, she had seen a man she had thought was Robson placing a gun very carefully against the side of the bedroom window. She would have called to him, but thinking that would only bring Annabelle out, she had decided to give up the idea of meeting him, and so had gone on to a village where she had to see about eggs, to learn that Annabelle Robson was murdered.

"Harold, you didn't love her!" she now said, almost pleadingly.

"I'm going to find out who killed her," he said to that. "And who crushed her face in like that?"

"I had nothing to do with that either I swear."

He gave her 'a long look.

"But you didn't love her!" she repeated "You didn't!"

"What did I tell you once before, when you said that?" he asked angrily.

"You don't! You didn't! You can't!" Her face was that of a fury.

"Why not? Don't you love Bramwell?" he asked shortly.

"No," she snapped back. "Oh, Harold—"

He held her off. She would have flung herself into his arms.

"Listen, Zilla. I did love Annabelle truly and I owed her everything—no man ever had a better mate. Would *you* have worked as hard as she did?" he demanded.

"No," was the instant reply. "But I'd have loved you better. She didn't know what love meant. I do."

He stepped away from her and leaned over the beside her, looking very tired and yet with eyes very bright.

"I wonder if you do!" he muttered "Anyway, going to marry Bramwell—"

"I'm not! Not now!" she breathed "I broke it off weeks ago."

He stood looking darkly at her.

"You're glad I'm not going to?"

He turned his face away.

"We must wait. I owe her that. No man ever had a better wife," 'he said hoarsely.

"She loathed you at the last," Zilla retorted.

"What?" he almost bleated. "Look here, Zilla, keep your tongue off Annabelle. We owe her that respect."

"I owe her nothing," she retorted with warmth, "except a jolly rude talk yesterday. She taunted me about being in love with you, and told me all you loved was money—which meant her, of course."

He stood silent, staring at her.

"Had you had heard her, you would have known dearly she loved you!" finished Zilla jeeringly.

"She was always jealous of you," he muttered excusingly. "She must have spoken in anger—"

"She wasn't angry with me yesterday," retorted Zilla, her dark eyes protruding, her face its ugliest. "She said she had been a fool over you, but she was cured of her folly."

"Annabelle said that!" Harold repeated. "I can't believe it!"

"She said you wouldn't believe it," Zilla retorted. "Said you seemed to think that once in love with you meant always in love with you, and no need for you to take any trouble."

"My God, you can hurt! I can't believe you! Why, we
never had one cross word! I don't say I didn't have to
struggle lest you bewitch me—but I did struggle. I won
out, and she never knew. Unless you told her." He
suddenly faced her again.

"There was nothing between us, but did you tell-her
there was?"

"No," she said, but she looked away from him. He eyed
her darkly.

"Oh, why take it like this?" she retorted, answering
some unspoken criticism. "I'm sorry now I came to you for
this talk. I thought—I thought—it was for me." She gave
a hard laugh.

"I loved Annabelle," he said simply. "I don't say with
the sort of love *you* can stir up in a man," he eyed her
sullenly, "but we were happy, and nothing you say—
nothing," he repeated, taking her wrist very firmly, "will
alter my knowledge that she loved me to the end. Just as
you were wrong in your monstrous thought that you saw
me, so you were wrong your understanding of what she
said to you yesterday."

"I'm not! I wasn't," she said. Then she looked into his
haggard eyes, and her face softened. "Oh, have it your
own way, then build a shrine to her if want to. And I'll
marry Bramwell and forget it!" She made as though to
turn on her heel. But he stopped her.

"Zilla, don't. One barrier has fallen without our doing.
Don't deliberately build up another to take its place."

"Then you *do* love me?" she said in a sweet beguiling
voice. Her face was very lovely. "I knew it! I knew it!"

"Zilla," he held her hand now, "don't let's go into it yet
awhile. All I ask is that you don't lock and bolt the gate
that may lead to another existence. But, at the moment,
there's only Annabelle's murder before me. Just one thing
I can do for her, and that's to find out who did it. Shut
your eyes, and think back to this afternoon, and tell me
everything you heard—every rustle you noticed—let
alone everything you saw."

She leaned against his shoulder, and this time he not did repulse her.

"I heard a door slam just a moment before the the shot came." Beyond that, so she said, she could remember nothing more.

"He must have been about my height," he went on. "I wonder if his being dressed like me was to take in Annabelle too, so that he could let himself into the house without her noticing him as he passed the window? Now, let's see, Whitehouse, and Green, are both my height . . . We are all three dark-haired. . . dark-eyed. . ." He bit his lip. "I shall be back early tomorrow morning, till then— there won't be any sleep for me till this horrible mystery is solved. I shall think, and you must think, and see if we can see any glimmer of light. I wish to God, though, that it hadn't been your coat found in the stove—it's hard to credit that you didn't go into the house—"

"Not so hard as to believe that it wasn't you at the window!" she retorted, with an ugly glint of teeth. Then a second later she had her arms around his neck. "Forgive me, that wasn't me, that was jealousy, that was my mouth that always speaks too quickly."

He unfastened her arms gently.

"I'm afraid we both have a lot to learn before we can work together, and work together we must to clear this up. Go home now, and let us try and have something helpful to suggest when we meet in the morning."

"And when do we meet and where?"

He was too tired to plan, and said she must leave it to chance. They would be sure to see each other, it must be frankly done, he wanted no hole-in-the-corner meeting, he said, and she pinched his arm.

"I'd meet you in the village sewer if need be," was her only comment.

"Not yet. Not like this," he said heavily, and she let him lead the way to the gate.

CHAPTER FIVE

Zilla did not know it, but it was a very relieved policeman who saw her get out of the train at Thoresway station. He had seen her catch the outgoing one, but had no orders to stop her.

Her mother was equally relieved to see her. She drew her at once into the sewing room, a seldom used nook.

"Zilla, about that leather coat of yours. The one Annabelle Robson passed on to you, the police have been asking about it."

"I know. It was found by them burning in the stove at The Clearing, when they were called in about the—about Annabelle's death."

"What?" Mrs. Ash went quite whiter "Oh God, no!"

Zilla looked at her with the inscrutable, almost contemptuous expression in her dark eyes which was so usual to them.

"How did it get there?" breathed her mother "Wait, I must call your father in. He must hear this,"

"I don't see any reason to make this a family party."

"There's every reason."

"The coat wasn't mine any longer. I had thrown it into the discard weeks ago—"

"Can you prove that?" asked her mother.

Zilla shook her head, and lit a cigarette.

Mrs. Ash fetched her husband. Closing the door behind her, she leaned with her back against it, and swiftly told him about the garment and the interest of the police in it.

Ash kept his eyes on his daughter, who, for her part seemed very bored.

"When did you throw the coat into the rubbish?" he demanded.

"Weeks ago. Over a month, to be exact."

"If anyone else saw it in the bin," her father slowly, "it would make an enormous difference. Someone might have—easily."

"Seeing that it has turned up in the stove at The Clearing I should say that it's evident someone did and fished it out," came the reply from Zilla.

"Could it have been used? I mean could anyone have worn it?"

"Oh dear, yes It was quite good still. Probably if it hadn't belonged to Annabelle, I shouldn't have thrown it away." Her tone was indifferent.

"Zilla," her mother spoke in a low, tense voice that no one had heard from her before. "Zilla, don't pose! If we're not careful, your whole life may be ruined. Once connect you—publicly—with Annabelle's—" She swallowed

"—death," said Zilla smoothly.

"It will always stand against you," finished her mother. "You know, we all know, what people will say, unless the mystery of that coat is cleared up!"

"Bramwell won't like it for one," said Asi heavily.

"It doesn't concern him. I've given him up."

"Where were you at midday today?" asked her mother in a whisper.

"Not far from The Clearing. Hoping I could have a word with Harold Robson before they left tomorrow."

Both her parents looked as though a bomb had exploded near them.

Neither spoke. Mrs. Ash sank into one of the chairs and put a hand to her forehead. Her husband stared at the floor. Then he repeated that everything must be done to try to find anyone who might have thrown something into the bin after Zilla had been to it, and who might have seen the coat.

"Harold is coming back tomorrow morning, he will be able to help us," Zilla said as though talking to children.

"Harold?"

"Harold Robson," Zilla explained She hesitated. "In due course, when all this is forgotten, we hope to marry.

That's quite confidential, of course," she said, as, waving her long cigarette holder in the air, she swept from the room, a triumphant smile on her lips.

"Good God!" said her father. "This is monstrous. It can't be allowed."'

Mrs. Ash followed her daughter into her bedroom, a very rare proceeding on her part.

"Zilla, this is madness," began Mrs. Ash.

"Very likely," said Zilla to that. "But who can help madness? Certainly not the person who's mad."

Something in her voice, in her face, so difficult to read, touched the mother. Then she shook off the softness.

"If you can't help it now, it's only because you made no effort to stop it in the beginning. You say Robson and you are going to be married. That's ridiculous. He won't marry you—and you know it."

"He won't marry me?" asked Zilla. "He asked me this afternoon to marry him, just as soon as he was free, as I always knew he would. Of course, not a word is to be said about our plans—yet a while."

Her mother stared at her with something like horror on her face.

"I hope this is another of your—inventions," she said finally. "You never worry to keep to the truth, if it doesn't appeal to you. I sincerely hope this is one of those occasions."

"Why should you hope that?"

"Why? With his wife just murdered in a ghastly way, with your coat found in the house, with your reputation for going to any lengths to get your own way, and with some who must know about your infatuation, which you've taken no pains to hide—if it's not known it's only thanks to Harold Robson, who, whatever you are making up, was known to be in love with Annabelle up to the end. My girl you may be up on a murder charge if you're not careful!"

Zilla began to polish her finger-nails.

"Thank God he was," said Mrs. Ash at last "that fact may keep people from talking for a while."

"Have it as you like," said Zilla carelessly. "But we don't intend to say anything about our plans, if that's any comfort. And we are both going all out to clear all this up."

When her mother left her alone, Zilla pulled a snapshot of Robson out of her drawer and looked at it for quite a long time.

Ash was standing in the doorway. He beckoned his wife to come in.

"l thought at first I wouldn't let you know, but it's all too serious . . . The coat that Zilla says she threw out weeks ago—I saw, it hanging in one the outhouses very recently."

"When did you see it?" Mrs. Ash whispered.

"This morning."

They looked at each other in silent dread. He recovered himself first.

"But this is nonsense, as if it mattered—I think I will tell Zilla that the coat was seen there. If I saw it, others may have. Of course, if it was there, we know that it was stolen one, but she should be warned—must be warned."

"Come with me," said Mrs. Ash, and once again went to her daughter's room. Zilla looked up in surprise.

Her father came to the point at once. She listened with no alteration in her face. Then she said casually, "Of course, if you saw it in the shed, then I must be mistaken in thinking I flung it out weeks ago. I meant to, but I do believe now that I kept forgetting it, and only got rid of it a few days ago."

"I saw it this morning, around nine," he said firmly. "This is a very important matter, don't just say the first thing that comes into your head. Think before you speak—for once in your life."

"Then it must have been today I threw it into the bin. Fact is, I didn't forget when it was, but I thought it would worry you to know. Personally, I don't see what damned difference it makes when I threw it away."

"The bins aren't cleared till tomorrow. Some-may have noticed the coat."

"Someone may have seen you put it in and have taken it out at once—to use . . ." Mrs. Ash spoke in a curiously dull tone.

For once Zilla looked thoughtful.

"Perhaps I'd better tell you. I didn't throw that coat away till lunch-time. I wore it when I went to The Clearing this morning. Oh, I didn't go in. I wanted a word with Harold if it could be had. But it was hot. I was tired of the thing, and, as I happened to pass the bin for leather and rubber throw-outs, I lifted the lid and flung it in.

Neither of her parents spoke.

"Let me see," Zilla seemed to calculate. "That would have been twelvish, or a little later. Between twelve and half-past let's say."

"Did anyone see you while you were wearing the coat?" asked her mother.

"I saw no one. I passed the gypsy caravans, but I saw none of the gypsies around. No, I don't think anyone saw me while I had it on, but, of course, I can't say for certain."

Her father picked up a book and slammed it back into place.

"Which version did you give the police?" he asked, not looking at her.

"Naturally that I threw the coat away weeks ago." .Zilla seemed surprised at the question.

The night was cold. Tyrwhitt smoked pipe after pipe in the depths of the car.

Suddenly, with no preliminary warning, a beam of light began to move along the road from the gate. It fell on his car and passed on without pausing. A police constable, Tyrwhitt thought, who had been told what to expect. But he did not like it.

It might not be the police at all. At any rate he was there, if any car should move out of the inn. He got out and stood staring at the garage doors, clearly visible in the moonlight. He thought, yes he was sure, that one was slightly ajar. The one in which the grey Lagonda was housed. A faint, very narrow, crack of light now showed in the blackout. He stood with one foot on his running board, the door of the car open, but nothing stirred. He looked at his watch. The luminous hands pointed to three o'clock. He waited two minutes, still the crack of light showed. Very cautiously he stole toward the door. He felt for the door's edge, so as to widen the streak of light; something crashed down on his head from behind.

Superintendent Clarkson spent a quiet, but a far from comfortable night. He had been in the bar, but neither of the men in whom he was interested had shown up. When it was time for him to hunt up the cubbyhole, he found a paper pinned on Whitehouse's door. It said "Do not wake me till lunch-time. No breakfast wanted." Green's door was unadorned.

"Umph," said Clarkson to himself "Perhaps it's just as well. Captain Tyrwhitt has the car handy. We shall see."

But he saw nothing and heard nothing out of the way. By eight o'clock next morning he thought he might consider the vigil over, and after a cup of tea went on to his home for a much needed wash and change.

He glanced in at the garage as he passed.. The Lagonda had not been moved. Outside, there was no sign of the police car. Evidently Tyrwhitt had considered eight o'clock the end of his vigil.

By the marks on the road, Clarkson could see where the car had turned and gone on in the direction towards the chief constable's house. He would find a report from Captain Tyrwhitt at the station.

But there was no report at the station. He ran up the chief constable's home. To his surprise, the maid told him "the Captain" had not come back yet.

"See if the green car, he was driving the Talbot, is back, there's a good girl," he requested urgently.

It was not there, he was told, and, on that, giving up all thoughts of bath or breakfast, he rang his chief.

"I'll go back to the White Hind, sir, at once, on my bike. Looks to me as though something had turned up that Captain Tyrwhitt's following. I'll have a word with Green, at any rate,"

Rushing along to the inn, Clarkson ran up the stairs, and tried the handle of Green's room. It was empty, but everything looked just as it had yesterday. Even the toothbrush was in its place. The soap and sponge were damp. Green might have gone out for a stroll, about the time that the superintendent was making for home.

He listened at the door of Whitehouse's room. It was very quiet. He tried the door. It was bolted on the inside. Unfortunately it looked on the front of the inn, so that any idea of a look in from a ladder against the sill had better be given up for the moment. Probably all was well.

Downstairs, he was told that that sign often adorned the writer's door, and that, equally often, Green would go for a morning walk before breakfast.

Clarkson strolled to the garage and quite automatically, from force of habit, opened the door of the grey car, and had a look inside. His mind was on Tyrwhitt's absence wondering where Tyrwhitt had got to. The reply lay before him.

In a second he had the young man out, and was cutting the clothes line that bound him, and getting the gag out of his cut mouth. A stiff drink of brandy from the superintendent's flask helped to restore Tyrwhitt's circulation as Clarkson kneaded and rubbed.

The lump on his head told the superintendent much of what had happened. As soon as he could speak, Tyrwhitt explained that he had not seen the man who struck him down.

"As soon as you can stand alone, I'll scout for ladder, and put it against the window and have look at Whitehouse's room," said Clarkson.

A few moments later, Tyrwhitt took a few groggy steps and, collapsing on a bench, told Clarkson that he was all right, and would be round at the door of Whitehouse's room as soon as the superintendent would be at the window.

Clarkson knew where a ladder was kept. In a trice he was up and over the sill of one of the open windows of Whitehouse's room. A moment later he let in Tyrwhitt.

Both went carefully over the room. Nothing of the late occupier's belongings had been left.

A tap came at the door. It was Robson who had just arrived back from his own home. An inquiry at the police station had told him that nothing fresh had so far been discovered. He had left the key of his house with them, and went on to the White Hind where he had got a room.

Robson, when he was shown up to his loom, had made himself comfortable, and then coming along for a word with his dead wife's cousin, had read the notice, but at the same time heard sounds of drawers being opened.

"Reg," he called, "you up?"

He was let in at once, and stared in silent amazement at the empty room and the two men going through the drawers.

When Robson was told of what had happened, he was tempted to tell the superintendent of the man who was seen by Zilla at the window with the rifle, the man whom she had taken for himself. Whitehouse and Green were both around his own height. Though there was no resemblance between any of them, yet neither of them had strikingly different features from his own. True, his own thick and curly hair was very different from either Whitehouse's thinning strands, or Green's light brown hair, but with a wig on, could either be mistaken for him? He thought they might be.

"What can have made him run away like this—if he has gone of his own free will?" he asked instead.

Clarkson told him that Whitehouse had not come out at all well in his interview at the police station.

Questioned on his account of the way that he had spent yesterday in Lincoln, he had contradicted himself badly. Alibis he had none apparently, except for Green's insistence that the two of them had been together all the time. Green had maintained that inquiries at the shops in question, and at the tea room, would bear out his time table. And, to a certain extent, this had proved to be the case. But no one could remember having seen Whitehouse with him.

Tyrwhitt and Robson went down the stairs, while Clarkson put the ladder back. He was joined by the two others, who had a look at the car where Tyrwhitt had spent so many more and more painful hours, and they stood a moment together taking in low tones of what had best be done now.

"You say that car of the chief constable's badly needs overhauling and so is none too easy to drive. Well, Whitehouse is a very poor driver, but Green can handle any car like a—"

He stopped, a telegraph boy was cycling up to the inn.

"Priority cable for Mr. Whitehouse, and one for—for—" he held out one to Robson.

It was addressed to his dead wife. Robson took them both and opened one at once. A glance at the contents and he passed it on to the police officer who in his turn handed it to Tyrwhitt. It was from the Biggers' solicitor in Canberra, and announced the death of Thomas Bigger in the Canberra hospital in the early hours of the night.

The cable to Whitehouse proved to be a duplicate.

There was no expression on Robson's face as he put the one he held carelessly into a pocket.

"I expected it yesterday," was all he said.

Clarkson and Tyrwhitt both wondered if Whitehouse had also expected it.

While Robson went on to use the telephone at The Clearing, Tyrwhitt made his way to his uncle's house, and had a hot bath and rub down, when Clarkson decided to chance Green's return, and go through his belongings.

A very careful and uninterrupted scrutiny showed nothing that could have any bearing on his disappearance, or on any crime. On the whole, Clarkson rather expected to see him again shortly.

Some quite simple accident might be detaining him, or a change of plan.

But Whitehouse . . . Clarkson hurried back to his station and there got in touch with the chief constable.

"I just had the tank filled up for captain Tyrwhitt," was the chief constable's first comment.

"With that he, or they, can have got to London."

"'Whitehouse couldn't do it before daylight," said Clarkson with certainty. "He's very cautious at the wheel in the blackout. I've sent out a call to stop the car, of course, sir, and to report having noticed its passage, and to pass that on to all garagemen."

"'Well, this simplifies our task," said Findlay. "Find Whitehouse and we find the murderer—apparently. Green's absence seems to be a mere accident."

"Looks that way, sir," agreed Clarkson. "I'm having a word with Acland. Mr. Robson says there's a good snapshot of them both at The Clearing, and we'll get the press here and in London to print it. Of course, we suppress the one of Green for the time being."

"Let's hope he'll turn up this afternoon, or give some sign of life."

It was just four hours later that Green rang up the superintendent. When Clarkson answered Green hailed him.

"Hello, Super, I'm on the trail of something really good. Don't expect me till you see me—with the proofs. I shall be back tomorrow, or the day after, at the outside."

"Where are you speaking from?"

"My secret for the time being. It's nothing the police can help in—only very much spoil. But
i don't want you to think I'm the escaped murderer."

"No, it's Mr. Whitehouse who has run away. Is he with you?"

"Good God! What do you mean? Surely he hasn't been such a fool!"

"His room is empty. So, we believe, is his bank account."

"You do surprise me!" There was no mistaking the mockery in the tones. "However, I must rush away," and the receiver at the other end slammed down.

Clarkson hurried out to see the chief constable.

"But for the fact that it couldn't be of any use to Green, I'd say he had a hand in the murder." Clarkson made no disguise of his dislike of the man.

"But the murder could be of use to Green," said Tyrwhitt. "He learns that Whitehouse is the next in line for the Australian fortune. The bit that went to Mrs. Robson, of course, would be out of his reach. Say Green decides that the money is worth two murders. First of Mrs. Robson, then of Whitehouse. He knows that Whitehouse will be suspected of the first murder, provided he is not allowed to have a good alibi. When Green was so carefully giving the impression that he was merely bolstering up Whitehouse in an attempt to create an alibi, suppose he was working to create just that effect—then he puts the wind still further up Whitehouse, who seems a bit of a rabbit—"

"Who, if your theory is true, is in a very unpleasant position," his uncle commented dryly. "Very unpleasant indeed. If he did return to The Clearing yesterday morning or midday—"

"Quite so, uncle. Green, in other words, has Whitehouse just where he wants him and is now keeping him in hiding, until from gratitude, or from fear of being given up, Whitehouse makes a will leaving everything to his faithful friend and secretary. After which Whitehouse meets with a fatal accident. Falls downstairs into the water . . . is run over by a car in the blackout . . . anyway, he will die. And, in due course, not immediately, of course—the Australian estate won't be wound up for months—someone finds Whitehouse's will, and Green, very surprised and touched, steps into the fortune . . . What about that for a neat, useful scheme, eh?"

"Very plausible," agreed his uncle.

"Of course he'd have to claim that he believed Whitehouse innocent," Clarkson continued, "or we'd be after him for bolstering Whitehouse's statements up with his story of having been with him all yesterday. Well, Captain Tyrwhitt, until something crops up to crack that theory of yours, quite a good one to work on. We've traced the telephone call to a booth in London, by the way."

"We sent the fingerprints of everyone connected with the murder to the Yard," said Findlay. "We may yet learn something from there. What was the idea of destroying Mrs. Robson's face though?" he asked his nephew. "Surely the last thing Green would want would be any doubt as to its being Annabelle Robson who was dead."

"I still think Miss Ash did that, Uncle—while wearing the leather coat. For no attempt was made really to destroy Mrs. Robson's identity. I think the damage to the face was just spite, and a woman's cruelty, showing itself. But, as Clarkson thinks, it might just possibly have been done by Green as the first step in a plan which he didn't have time to carry out."

"Either way doesn't matter," said Findlay "What we want is to get hold of those two men."

"I don't think Green will stay in London, sir," said Clarkson now. "He's apparently lived there a lot, which would mean the danger of coming across someone who would recognise him . . . I should expect he'd take himself—and Whitehouse—to some other large town. What about a word with Miss Margaret Ash? She does extra secretarial work for Whitehouse since the accident to her foot, and may think of some place he would want to make for."

"I'll ask the various chief constables to have their men comb all the big hotels. In descriptions, I'll stress the probability of disguise."

"Make an appointment with Mr. Horton, Whitehouse's bank manager in Lincoln, for me around eleven," he said in an aside to Clarkson as he picked up the telephone.

"Very good, sir. He's a personal friend of Whitehouse's."

"Indeed! I shall let a little of Captain Tyrwhitt's theory—which is the police theory now—leak out. Enough to let him see that we are worried about Whitehouse's safety. You, Geoff, might talk to Margaret Ash, and do the same. In strict confidence, and without saying that we agree with you, of course. But worry her about Whitehouse. By the way," he turned to Clarkson, "you found nothing among Mrs. Robson's things at The Clearing, that can help us, I suppose?"

"Nothing whatever, sir."

The little meeting broke up on that. Tyrwhitt was lucky enough to find Margaret in and alone. She was typing out some figures very carefully.

"My father's down at the stables—" she began.

"I didn't come to see him, but to have a talk with you about Mr. Whitehouse." Tyrwhitt looked around him as though to assure himself that they were really alone, before he continued "I've something to tell you—in very strict confidence—about Mr. Whitehouse—"

Margaret's deep-set, tranquil eyes widened. Tyrwhitt told her of his disappearance.

"But—but—" she almost stammered. "Why should he do such a thing? You don't suspect him, surely, of having had anything to do with his cousin's dreadful end?"

"Don't you?" Tyrwhitt asked, instead of replying.

"Oh no! No! Impossible! For a man of his character. And he's fond of Annabelle—"

"Well, there is this possibility—" and Tyrwhitt sketched his own theory.

He found that Margaret did not in the least exclaim at the impossibility of Green being a criminal. On the contrary, she too thought that he had grasped the right end of the tangled string leading to the heart of the mystery.

"But the face? The burnt coat?" Margaret asked in a hushed voice that suggested that she held those two points in particular horror.

Tyrwhitt briefly gave his uncle's idea of an interrupted crime Then he returned to the subject of Whitehouse, and the danger that he might be in at this very moment. Could Margaret suggest any possible place he might prefer as a hiding place?

Margaret could not help, but she felt certain, she said, that if able, he must get into touch with her shortly.

"You've told me something in confidence, I'll tell you something too," she said, sitting back and nursing her foot. "Mr. Whitehouse isn't writing novels at the moment. He's a first class mathematician, and it's in the applying of mathematics to practical problems that he seems to specialize. Something very important is in hand just now, or rather has been, since he came to The Clearing. He's writing a book on ballistics for the War Office. I've been helping to type out the references, which is all that I am capable of. Mr. Green does the typing of the actual text, he's an extremely able man. But what I want to say is that, in view of the importance of his work, and the fact that I've got the list of references used in his last section all but complete, Mr. Whitehouse is sure to get into touch with me very soon. I know his last section is nearly ready, and that the special publishers are waiting for it."

"You don't think that Green's absence might have nothing to do with Mr. Whitehouse, and that Mr. Whitehouse has been kidnapped by someone else who wanted to stop his work?" she asked suddenly.

"Where would the murder of Mrs. Robson come into that?" asked Tyrwhitt, and she did not insist.

It was agreed that should Whitehouse communicate with her in any way, she would at once let Tyrwhitt, or the police, know.

CHAPTER SIX

Chief Inspector Pointer looked through the papers on his desk this Monday morning. Scotland Yard was very short-handed, and he had to be his own clerk. He quickly sorted them out after one glance. Then he rang a number up on the telephone and asked for Superintendent Bolting; was told that he was out on a case, and had not yet reported back.

"Then I'll go around at once. A dead body has been found in a flat in Brompton Road which is believed to be a suicide." He added a few details and hurried out to the police car.

He had the morning paper with him. It was full of the latest development of The Clearing murder as it was called. Pointer had not yet read it. Instead he reviewed the facts on the dead body which he was about to see.

A young man had been found, dead in his furnished room in Halkin Street. On the table a half sheet of paper had been found on which was written "I have taken the only way out, G. Morris."

The caretaker of the flats had found the body and sent for the police. A doctor happened to be in the house at the time and had said that the man appeared to have died the night before last.

The car stopped. Pointer got out and slipped swiftly into the front door. The suite into which he was shown was on the ground floor and consisted of two large, well-furnished rooms and a bathroom. A constable was waiting for the chief inspector. The body of a man fully dressed lay on the bed. He looked about thirty.

Another police car arrived bringing the police. A word with Pointer, and he took the temperature of the body, examined it swiftly, and smelled the mouth. He glanced at a bottle without on any label on it lying on the floor, as though it had fallen from the dying hand, smelled it too, and nodded.

"Been dead over twenty-four hours I should say, offhand. Poison. One of the Atropine groups." He sniffed at the hair, and ran a lock through his fingers. "Permanent wave. Hair-setting lotion." He glanced at the clothes. "Well, I mustn't encroach on your preserves—"

"Shoot anything you'd like," said Pointer equably.

Obviously expensive, rig-out . . . manicured . . . never done an hour's work in his life. Yet he chose about as painful a way out as he could. Well, I must be off," and he hurried out.

Pointer had a long look at the body as it lay on the bed. It had obviously been an agonising death. The features, like the convulsed body, said as much.

Curious that with a war on, a man should choose this end. . . . He looked at the written sentence. Then he asked the constable about the house. He learned that it had a very good record. Next, he saw the caretaker. The suite had been empty for about three days when the dead man had come to look at it about a year ago. He had taken it at once, given his bank as reference, and sent in the carpets the next day. The furniture had followed. All new and expensive, from one of the best known furnishing houses in town. Obviously the dead man had not been in money difficulties. He was often away, having a home in Sussex, and only using the suite when he had to be overnight in town. The staff only came in by day. Yesterday being Sunday, no one had gone into the dead man's suite. At night the caretaker was alone in his rooms in the basement. The house door was shut at eleven, but all the occupiers had keys. No meals were served in the house, except breakfast by request.

The ambulance was called and the body was taken out quickly on a covered stretcher. The porter was shocked.

"He seemed such a cheerful bloke."

Pointer and he both glanced involuntarily at the paper on the table.

"Would you say that was his handwriting?" asked Pointer.

The porter had never seen his writing, except on his checks, and could not say.

When he had left, Pointer looked through the contents of the pockets which he had emptied and listed before letting the body go. A bunch of keys, the stubs of two matinée tickets for the stalls of the last day of July—a Saturday. This was now the ninth of August. A note case with over six pounds ten in it, a gold cigarette case initialed G. M., a handkerchief with a laundry mark, a fountain pen, a cigarette lighter and some eight shillings of loose change completed the lot.

Pointer went over the room very carefully. Nearly twenty suits of clothing, underwear, all of good quality, racks of shoes, and among other things, a check book on a bank in Lowndes Square.

Pointer rang up the bank and asked for an interview with the manager. Within five minutes he had walked around the corner, and been shown into the office of the bank in question. The manager seemed very surprised, as well as shocked at the news of his customer's death.

"We've had his account for some three years. He has another at our Head Office in the City. Well-to-do young man. Self-made, but a very pleasant type. Owns a chain of hair-dressing shops in town and in the country. Whatever the cause of his death, I can only say that it wasn't due to financial troubles. And I can't help wondering whether it wasn't an accident. He was in here only"—he glanced at his engagement pad—"last Saturday—and you think he died that night?"

"Looks like it, so far."

"Well, I can assure you that he wasn't hinting of death on Saturday morning. He's a cheerful chap, always ready to laugh and see a joke. Thorough going optimist as is—was—natural, seeing how well he was doing himself. We have his will. I know the contents. Everything to named charities, bar a hundred to myself."

Pointer asked whether the dead man had had an office in the City and was given an address there. Also that of his house at Hailsham in Sussex, and the name of his only relative, a brother, whom the dead man had repeatedly helped, but who was a drunken sot.

"Mr. Morris was clearing about eighteen hundred a year at the moment, and spending around a thousand all told. The Head Office of our bank manages his I.T. returns. A very straightforward fellow, in every way, I found him," said the manager.

Pointer returned to Halkin Street, and sent a constable for the brother, whose address was near Victoria. He was not in. Then he looked for the dead man's telephone book. He could not find one, nor any form of address book, but, at the last, noticing a small knob on the foot of the telephone, pulled on it, and drew out a kind of patent double leaf, on which the dead man had apparently put a list of names and their telephone numbers. He looked through the names, listing them all. Mostly they were of business, but tthere were a few which, from the addresses, looked like being those of friends. One such name was Robson. Robson! . . . A murdered woman in Lincoln, a dead man here in London. It is by no means an uncommon name, but Pointer put through a special call from the nearest police station to the Chief Constable of Lincoln and then, as he was not in, the Superindent of Thoresway.

There he had better luck. Pointer asked whether name of a Mr. Morris—George Lever Morris full—had turned up at all in connection with any the people linked with The Clearing case. Superintendent Clarkson said that it had not. Pointer asked Clarkson where he could get in touch, just to make sure, with Robson himself.

He was told that Robson was in town at the moment, staying at Bailey's Hotel, off Cromwell Road. Pointer put a call through to Robson. "Morris?" said Robson's voice . .

. "Yes, my wife had an acquaintance of that name, or rather, an old acquaintance who turned up again. What's wrong with him? Car accident?" Pointer asked whether Mr. Robson would be so kind as to see him, as soon as he could get to the hotel. Robson, sounding mystified, said he would be in the lounge. Snapshots were being developed of Morris in the dead man's bathroom. He took the clearest, folded all wet in blotting paper, with him. After explaining to Robson the reason for the Yard being interested in Morris, Pointer showed him the print. Robson nodded. "Good God! How horrible! That's the man!" He went on to explain that one evening about two months ago, some friends of his wife's family had asked them both with Whitehouse to the Savoy for dinner, and they had stayed the night in town. It turned out to be the night of one of London's worst air raids. Hurrying in through the main doors of their hotel, amid a crowd of others, caught like themselves, this man Morris had been literally catapulted into their midst. He and his wife had recognized each other with some mutual amusement, and the four, the newcomer, Whitehouse and his wife, and Robson had kept together in a group downstairs in the shelter. He seemed an agreeable, cheery fellow, and was a great friend of some Australian friends of Mrs. Robson's. It was at their London home that Morris and his wife had met. They had all exchanged cards, and he and his wife had asked Morris to look them up, should he ever be in Lincolnshire. Morris had promised to do this, and they had given a similar promise about his house at Hailsham. The raid had then petered out, and Morris had been able to get away to his own rooms.

Pointer asked for the name of the mutual friends. Robson said that he had forgotten it for the moment. They were not people known to himself, but to his wife and also, he thought, to her cousin Whitehouse. A good deal of the time he and Whitehouse were watching the wonderful sight of the lit-up sky from the front steps, and so he had lost much of the talk between Mrs. Robson and Morris.

"What a strange fatality that he should be dead too," said Robson "They were the merest acquaintances—fate is odd—"

When Pointer got back to the Yard, he found the autopsy report waiting for him. Morris had been dead at least thirty hours. He had died from atropine poisoning. The poison was almost impossible for a layman to obtain, except in the form of eye drops. But he would have had to drink at least twenty of the ordinary sized eye drop bottles to account for the quantity found in him. The poison had been taken in one draught—as a man would do who wanted to kill himself. Morris had a very weak heart, but, apart from this, was in good health and clearly had lived in comfortable circumstances.

Pointer had a word with one of his men, and decided to go to Morris' office. He found that the original one had had a direct hit, and Morris had secured a small room in a large building, with an outer office shared with four other firms. The war staff in the outer room consisted of two women, an elderly secretary and a girl typist.

Pointer asked the lift man about any people who came to see Morris. He was told that as a rule Morris had quite six or seven callers on every day that he was at his office, which was about three times a week. The lift man knew many of them by sight. Pointer asked him if a young lady had called within the last two months.

The man thought a moment and then nodded.

"Once. Never called here before. Wasn't sure of the number of his office. . . Quite young. Very handsome gal. . . .Fair, and a bit painted, but a lady all right."

As to when she had come—close on two months ago, he couldn't be certain of the date, but felt sure it was not longer than eight weeks at the outside.

Pointer asked who showed visitors into the office. Whichever of the typists was in the outer office at the time, he was told.

He, himself, was now taken up, and stepped into the large room off which the four smaller rooms opened. There was only the secretary there at the moment.

In reply to his questions, she said Mr. Morris had had a young lady to see him some weeks just the once. But she had not been the one to see her. However, if he would wait, Miss Fraser would be back from taking notes. Pointer waited and talked about Morris, who seemed to have been very much liked here too. They all knew of his having been found dead in his rooms.

"He took the stuff by mistake. That much is certain," said the secretary.

Miss Fraser now entered, and flung her notebook on the table.

Pointer was introduced as from Morris' solicitors.

"It's about a lady—young—who called to see Mr. Morris close on eight weeks ago. We want a word with her, and can't find her address. Did you see her?"

"That's right. I showed her in. Was he surprised? I'll say he was!"

"What was she like? It may not be the same lady as the one we wanted to trace. Can you describe her?"

"Very fair. Beautifully done hair. She blacked her eyebrows and lashes. And her clothes! Gosh, her hat alone would cost me a month's pay. She wore a short white lambskin coat, pleated white crepe-de-chine skirt— black gloves and hat, black and white shoes—and her bag must have cost a fortune. That bag alone . . ."

"Do you remember the name?"

Evidently this was considered a trifle compared with the outfit. But Miss Fraser thought hard. Then her face cleared.

"I know! It was the same as the name in the papers this morning, in The Clearing Murder . . . You know— Robson! That's it. Mrs. Robson it was."

"Well, that's a step forward. Mrs. Robson, you say? Did she send in her name, then?"

The girl nodded. "Told me to say it was 'Mrs. Robson to see him.' They were old friends, evidently."

"Ah!" Pointer looked very portentous. "That's what we think too. Now, we haven't been able to trace any other old friends of Mr. Morris'. Where is his address book, by the way?"

"There's only business names in the one he has here."

"I see. But now, about Mrs. Robson. Do you know her Christian name by any chance?" She did not.

"How long did this lady stay?"

"Oh, ever so long! They seemed to have a great deal to talk over and laugh about." The typist said that Mr. Morris seemed in high good humor as he took the lady—Mrs. Robson—down in the lift. He and she must have gone on to tea together, because it was quite an hour later that he came back.

"Did she only come the once?"

"That's all."

"But she would telephone him?"

Both women were certain that she had never used the telephone.

"Now when, exactly, was this visit of hers?"

After a talk between themselves, they fixed it definitely as two days after the last bad air raid. That meant eight weeks ago.

Pointer learned nothing more, and left them still chanting Morris' praises.

Back at the Yard, he found Bernard Morris, the brother of the dead man, waiting for him. Bernard was a short stocky man of around forty in a gunner's uniform. He was taken to see the body, and identified it at once as that of his only, and younger, brother.

Brought back to the chief inspector, he said that George had been apprenticed as a boy to a hairdresser, had done very well and risen to be a manager, then was made manager over several shops by a well-known company. Next, he had bought up one of the company's smaller places, and from that, had gone steadily upward.

"He must be making over a thousand a year," said Bernard bitterly. "But a fat lot of interest he takes in me! Wouldn't you think that with all that money a man would give a hand to his only brother?"

Pointer recalled him. Where had his brother lived?

"A year ago he had sought the New Manor House at Hailsham in Sussex. A beautiful house, according to Bernard, with a great big garden and all. Two cars mind you, and in with all the nobs. Joined the tennis club, first thing, and the golf club. He keeps his business to himself, did George. Who comes in for all his property, Mister? He wasn't married."

Pointer again brought him back to the brother himself.

"Was he the type to commit suicide, would you think?"

"I'm not surprised to hear of what's happened," said Bernard with relish. "Stands to reason that sort of thing can't be done honestly. No, I'm not surprised at anything you could tell me about George. But I think it was the last calling up notice what really did it. He'd dodged the army for quite a while, while older men with not half his strength did their bit. Got a doctor to certify him as a weak heart . . . wonder how much he paid him for that weak heart?"

"When did you see him last? I thought you said he and you did not see much of each other?"

"Not if he could sidestep me. But about a fortnight ago I ran into him, see, and he had to stand me a drink, and part with a couple of quids. Do you know, I didn't even know where he hung out in town? Not until I read it in the noon paper. He had just had another calling up notice served on him, at Hailham, and wasn't he worked up about it, and all!"

"You know of nothing else, except that, which would account for his having taken his life?"

Bernard again began to generalize, and to guess.

"Had he any special friend or friends?"

"None. Never wanted anyone to get close to him."

Pointer handed him over to a constable to take down his statement and looked up the trains to Hailsham.

Hailsham yielded nothing of interest. There was no record of the Robsons in the large, well-furnished house, and such friends as Morris had down there were all recent ones.

Pointer caught the evening train back to the Yard. There he found that the Lincolnshire chief constable had been trying to get him some three times.

Pointer was promptly put through to Major Findlay.

"It's about the name of Morris," said that officer at once. "I'm sorry I was out when you rang up. As a matter of fact, it has just now cropped up in The Clearing murder. Have you seen the report of it in today's papers?"

Pointer said that he had.

"You remember that one of the Ash sisters, who were friends of Mrs. Robson, said that Mrs. Robson had been getting a book ready to send off when she arrived?"

"Yes."

"Well, when I asked her about Morris just now, she recollected that that was the name on the book that Mrs. Robson had wrapped up and placed by the clock. She didn't see the name on the package but Mrs. Robson pressed it down on the clean blotter, and it stood out clearly for she had written in block capitals. She says it was only when I put to her that the memory of the blotter came up, and of the name stamped on it. The initial was G. or might have been part of an 0. The address was blurred."

"The top sheet of blotting paper was taken away, wasn't it?" Pointer asked.

"It was. Have you seen the records?"

"No, sir. But as the name of Morris had turned up so far in the case, that seemed likely. May I have a copy of all The Clearing murder records sent to me?"

Major Findlay promised that this should be done immediately.

"This Morris affair strikes another odd note. The case is full of them. We believe on the whole that Green did it, but there are such a lot of unexplained odds and ends. I shall be very glad to be kept informed about your Morris investigations."

"Certainly, sir," said Pointer

The next on the telephone was Robson. He had just remembered the name of the mutual friend of Morris and his wife as Miller. The Millers decided to go back home to Australia in the beginning of the war, but stopped on in Singapore, as the father had a good deal of money invested in Jahore. There they were submerged by the Japan attack, and father, mother and daughter are presumed as missing, presumably killed by enemy action."

Robson said his wife told him the Millers had a daughter. Her name was Ada, he thought, but Mrs. Robson said she was always called Posey, and also that Morris had been very much in love with Ada—or Posey—when she had met him.

Pointer asked about the book which it was now known Mrs. Robson had done up, addressed to Morris, and put on the mantel.

Robson said he had no idea what had become of it, but knew, that his wife intended sending one to Morris. He seemed to remember that she had said it was the anniversary of the Miller girl's birthday.

Next morning Pointer had a long talk with the assistant commissioner.

"You think the suicide may be connected with The Clearing murder?" said that official thoughtfully. "You don't think the local police are right in their reading of the riddle?"

"It leaves a lot unexplained," said Pointer slowly.

"Are you suggesting that there is some link between Mrs. Robson and Morris other than that she gave? And that her murder was the cause of his suicide?"

"That's the stand I shall take, sir," said Pointer

"Ah," the chief assistant commissioner studied Pointer in silence for a moment. "I see. I wish they had called us in over The Clearing, murder!" The assistant commissioner spoke regretfully, "Interesting case. They've sent you a copy of all the evidence, I hear. What do you yourself think is the most significant piece, so far to hand?"

"The request for the dog. I can't help feeling that if that were understood—a great deal of the crime would be clear."

"Rats, or a burglar that she heard stirring about?" suggested the other, making squiggles on his blotting pad.

"Surely Ash, the father, would have been a nervous person's choice. And Mrs. Ash said her voice was almost unrecognizable and shaking badly.

"If Mrs. Ash is reliable, and everyone seems to think she is, then I, too, grant fright, sir. Only I don't think the reason of that fright is necessarily covered by either rats or burglars."

"Well, have a try at the compound puzzle then, for that's what you're really after, I know. But you'll have to do it in your spare time, as it were. I can't let you take up your official residence in Lincolnshire; however keen you are on it."

"On finding why Morris killed himself, sir," corrected Pointer.

The assistant commissioner snorted.

CHAPTER SEVEN

When he returned to his own rooms at the Yard, after the interview with the assistant commissioner, Pointer, was surprised to see a tall, slender man in khaki rising from a chair outside his inner office. Tyrwhitt introduced himself. He had come up to town on an Army matter, but his uncle had asked him to have a talk with the chief inspector as well.

"I dropped in to ask if you could have lunch with me at my club?" Tyrwhitt said, as they shook hands.

The chief inspector had to stipulate for rather a late hour, but after being assured that any time would suit, they parted to meet again later in the latter's Service Club, where they had a quick meal washed down with really good beer.

"I left word for us to be disturbed only in case of a telephone message," said the Army man. "Now Chief Inspector, you have had all the reports about The Clearing murder. As far as I'm concerned the case is at a standstill for the time being, but what about your man's suicide? Do you want a volunteer?"

"For what?" asked Pointer.

"To help you unwind your bit of stuff," said Tyrwhitt. "I've seen the beginning from one end, I'd like to see its continuation from the other end. Supposing I'm right, and you are going to link our murder and your suicide."

Pointer made no reply for a full minute.

"Hope you don't mind my butting in," said Tyrwhitt with his disarming grin. "Of course, I grant Mrs. Robson's murder is a dozen puzzles rolled into one."

"A dozen puzzles? There's no such thing, Captain Tyrwhitt, in a criminal case." Pointer's tone robbed his words of any suspicion of a lecture. "A crime is one and indivisible. Oh, I don't say that extraneous oddments may not get in here and there, but the greater part of what seem scattered bits, must all belong to a correct solution—be part of it, be quite intelligible, even to be seen to be necessary, by its light."

"The telephone summons for the dog—the crushed features—the burnt coat?" queried Tyrwhitt. "They're outside our present solution. We think the two last must be put to Miss Ash's account."

"But I thought she was a handsome girl?"

"She is, to some people's way of thinking. Not mine. Robson preferred his wife, and thought her prettier. But what have looks to do with it?"

"You think she was jealous of the dead woman's beauty. It's asking a lot to believe that any young woman would mutilate the face of even her most envied and most successful rival. Unless she herself were extremely ugly." Pointer was thinking aloud. "There wasn't only one blow with the hod, remember. Four times it must have been brought down, laden with coal, and smashed with full force on to Annabelle Robson's upturned face. It takes a very strong motive—and a very unusual character to fit with that act."

"Miss Ash is an unusual woman," said Tyrwhitt stoutly. "I've made inquiries, and, besides being madly in love with Robson as we know, they say she has the temper of the devil when roused."

"She'd have to have his character, as well as his temper, to have done that," was all Pointer said.

"You think the face, and the coat, and the asking for the dog are all parts of the actual murder?"

"They seem to me to be integral parts of the crime," said Pointer. "I put the sending for the dog on one side, for the moment. There seems no reason to think that there were two people concerned in the murder, yet the face was crushed immediately after that blow on the back of the head, the blow that split her skull. Yet I think it's asking too much to think that someone, not the murderer, came in, and used the hod as it was used the very instant after the woman was killed with the hatchet, yet didn't see the blow struck and so wasn't an accessory. There's no evidence to show that Miss. Ash and Green were extra friendly, is there?"

"The general belief is the other way," Tyrwhitt replied, "but that means little. We know now that the man she is engaged to broke off the engagement and has married another woman. That looks as though he had learned of something going on. My uncle is looking all that up, of course. He has a sister-in-law who knows the girl this Bramwell has married. Bramwell's mother talks of Zilla Ash as though she were Messalina herself.

"Look here," Tyrwhitt leant forward confidentially. "Do you link that clean blotting-paper pad with Morris because his name was marked on it? But that would mean that he was of great importance in the crime. And clearly he was not."

"The paper he left behind might be read as a confession of guilt," Pointer reminded him.

"Oh, surely that's not possible! He's quite unknown at Thoresway. His name has never cropped up before . . . he stands to gain nothing by her death. . ."

Pointer said nothing, only studying his shoe tips as though fascinated by something he saw there. He, too, did not for a moment believe that Morris had murdered Mrs. Robson.

"By the way," went on Tyrwhitt, "I don't think anyone told you about the button off the leather coat which I found under the telephone. It's of no importance as we know all about the coat."

Pointer questioned him about his find.

"Doesn't stand for anything fresh, of course," said Tyrwhitt when he had told him all the details.

"It might stand for everything," said Pointer, "it shows that there was a quarrel in that room, a bitter one, to tear a leather coat."

"But the room itself was in perfect order," said Tyrwhitt, "as is noted in the record of what we found when we arrived."

"The room versus the button, eh? Then the quarrel was localized. In other words, only centered on the coat itself, or, possibly, something in its pockets."

"The missing sixty pounds? At first Robson thought they were the reason for the murder, even still he thinks they were taken by the murderer."

"Everything was done quickly, we know," said Pointer, thinking aloud. "A brief struggle, but a fierce one—"

"With the wearer of the coat?" suggested Tyrwhitt.

"To tear off the throat button . . . you saw Miss Ash very shortly afterwards, and she showed no bruises? No swollen neck or cheek?"

"Nothing showed on her, or on any of the men," replied Tyrwhitt. "No roughhouse look about any of the lot. Evidently the coat had to be destroyed we know."

"But it wasn't destroyed! Whoever put it in the stove must have known it would take a long time to burn right up." Pointer considered this a very important difficulty. "It had evidently to be burned, yes, but apparently only enough to prevent something, some mark on it, some name perhaps, being found."

"While I'm at a loose end, until we get on Green and Whitehouse's tracks, or rather single track, may I be allowed to be a humble follower of your hounds on foot?" asked his companion.

"The difficulty would be official," Pointer explained. "In trying to find out why, a wealthy, cheery man should have killed himself, I may have to touch on the other case . . . if I believe that his suicide was because of the murder, of Mrs. Robson, I must more than touch it."

"And so you intend to hold firmly that her death was the reason for his taking poison. I get it!" said Tyrwhitt joyfully. "I'm with you every step of the way. But between ourselves, haven't you forgotten 'Posey'!"

"'Posey' might be Mrs. Robson's nickname, for aught we know," was the quiet answer.

Tyrwhitt laughed. "There's nothing like sticking to one's guns," he agreed. "But I think you'll have your work cut out to find anything in Mrs. Robson's past to account for her death making your man kill himself. Well, unofficially we have among ourselves just glanced at the thought of Robson and Zilla Ash: Zilla whose coat, if found, would have had to be destroyed. Say he discovered she had left it behind her after clearing off, but then his story would be a fabrication—and if so why did he kill his dog? Besides, putting aside all question of affection between the Robsons; the murder a wife could surely have been much better planned by any husband, and carried out far more easily, and without rousing any suspicion. Then too, his knowledge that a few days would bring that huge fortune here only Whitehouse, and therefore Green fit. What about Whitehouse and Zilla?"

"Possible," Pointer conceded. "So is Green and Zilla Ash. Frankly, to me, the whole crime suggests a mad rush, someone to whom a day's delay would, or might, make all the difference."

"As though the murderer rushed the murder through in the short time between the wife's telephone message and the husband's arrival in a car? It's the only time that Robson had left The Clearing for any length of time during their visit. We think the murderer may have planned the crime when he thought Robson was away in Gainsborough for a whole day, and a whole night, and then learned that Robson had come back that same afternoon?" Tyrwhitt ended on a questioning tone.

"Certainly a strong presumptive case can be made out against Whitehouse, or Green, preferably the former," Pointer conceded.

Tyrwhitt knocked out his pipe. "By the way, we're getting your aid about locating the missing men. The commissioner had promised to have police look into all arrivals of two men within the last few days. He thinks they'll make for a large hotel. Incidentally, Robson is working at his cousin papers for any clue as to where the two might go first. What are you going to do first?"

"Turn the whole over in my mind," said Pointer, "and if you can be of any help, I'll let you know at once."

"Thanks for the kind dismissal," Tyrwhitt rose with a good-natured smile.

When he was alone, Pointer lit his pipe, and walked his room. Was money again the answer to the riddle, as it is in almost every murder, though that murder is often listed under quite another heading? Green or Whitehouse would answer in that case, but the shooting at Robson was not clearly indicated, nor why the murderer, so pressed for time, had had to burn Mrs. Robson's coat. There Zilla Ash alone fitted . . . apparently, but she did not fit the shooting at Robson, nor did she, to his mind, explain the mutilation of the face immediately the woman had been struck down. That destroyed face, the blank blotting pad, and—yes—the death of Morris, could all be regarded as making one coherent group, but it seemed far-fetched to think that, because of a book sent to him, Morris had been killed. His name was known since the night in the Savoy shelter . . . could it be that 'Posey,' first mentioned apparently on that fly leaf, had a meaning here? It seemed rational to assume that the link which he felt sure connected the two deaths was one that centered around Annabelle herself.

For the moment then, it was Annabelle Robson herself on whom all his mind centered The over-worked woman whom Whitehouse had been able to help with the check from her parents in Australia would not have had much time in which to lead a second, hidden life. It was no use speculating on the reason for her request for a dog in the house, beyond believing that in some way it was connected with what befell her not an hour later. The reason for the murder, unless Green was the man, must have its roots in a part of her life unknown as yet. The Annabelle Robson here, of these papers—Pointer tapped

the thick envelope—could not have given any man any
reason to do away with her, let alone crush her face out
of all human semblance. Somewhere in her life must lie
the root of that terrible flowering. But when had she had
any time for growing wild roots? Not in Australia? She
had married at eighteen. All agreed too much in believing
her to have been unusually in love with her husband for
it not to have been true. Yet somehow—at some time . . .
And Morris? If his death was connected with that of
Annabelle Robson, did it come in here? Even assuming as
a starting point the easy answer of a man killing himself
because the woman he loves was dead, where did he fit
in? Whatever his own ideas of the death of the
prosperous, cheerful business man, Pointer intended to
start on the romantic suicide theory, which presupposed a
link between him and Annabelle Robson. But when could
it have been forged? That meeting at the Savoy, which
Robson seemed to have assume was accidental, was it
quite different?' Or was it really a chance meeting and yet
one that brought death to the woman? To his mind,
cheery Morris was a very unusual type of murderer, in
spite of popular opinion that there is no such type. In any
case a murder must mean a depth of feeling, whether
hatred, thwarted passion—presume it to be what you
will—for which there seemed no place in the life story of
Annabelle Robson—so far as it was known. How far was
that? It seemed very complete, but was there some gap—
some interval in which an unknown Annabelle Robson
could have taken command? Pointer got out the papers
and again studied them carefully. It looked to the chief
inspector as though he might, on the whole, be building
too much on Morris' acquaintance with the murdered
woman.

Pointer checked over the police records of the Robsons'
movements before buying The Clearing. Practically every
week seemed accounted for, and there was no record of
Morris ever having been to Wales in the three years

during which the Robsons had lived there after their
arrival in the British Isles.

Was there then only some slight, however romantic
acquaintance connecting Morris and Annabelle Robson?
Was his death, even if a murder, unconnected with hers?
Pointer did not think so. He believed that the two were
linked in death, and so had been linked in life.

Once again he mentally ran over all the known facts
of Annabelle Robson's short life. He reviewed the facts of
Green and of Whitehouse's statements in connection with
her. Green seemed quite out of it. There was just one
place in Whitehouse's story . . . just a bare possibility . . .
he decided to go to Thoresway and see if he could find
anything to turn the possibility into a probability.

Today was, he knew, the day of Annabelle's funeral.
The inquest had been held the previous afternoon and
had been adjourned for a fortnight. Pointer waited at
Thoresway station until the very few passengers had
gone on their way. He was to learn later, from the chief
constable, that the funeral had been very quiet. Mr. and
Mrs. Ash were there, but Margaret Ash's foot had got
infected and she was in a nursing home. Zilla Ash could
not get the day off, so she said, and had carried on with
her work as usual. Robson had looked very worn and
grim, but had shown no sign of any emotion throughout
the service. Acland had been there as a reporter, and had
watched everything with that cool detachment of his.
Clarkson, Major Findlay, and Tyrwhitt had all gone, as in
duty bound to represent the police.

When Pointer got to Thoresway, not one of it
mourners was to be seen about in the village. Life had
resumed its usual clothes and routine. Pointer explained
to the ticket collector that he want to go on to Curtain
Lindsey, but he thought he could do the last bit quicker
by bus. He was told that he could, but that the next bus
would not start til noon. He seemed at a very loose end,
till he suddenly bethought him aloud of The Clearing and
the murder. The ticket collector was able and willing to

have a glass of beer. "I think I must have met Mrs. Robson once in the train to Lincoln," said Pointer, evidently in a reminiscent mood, "she had come back from some visit. As I saw, from the case, I think it might have been just around the time that cousin Mr. Whitehead—"

"Whitehouse—"

Pointer accepted the lapse of memory and waited for a comment on his words.

"But Mrs. Robson never traveled anywhere—not in those days," said the ticket collector. "Things changed afterwards, I'll say they did! But not those days. She couldn't have afforded even a bus."

Pointer looked puzzled, "But I saw her more than once. Not to talk to, you know, but it was her all right. During that first fortnight after that cousin of hers got here, it was. I wondered they didn't talk at the inn of her being away, I don't think I can be wrong." But the man scoffed so at the idea that, if Pointer's theory had any foundation in fact at all, Mrs. Robson had not left her home, or returned to it, by train. He drifted into the village shop but the postmistress turned out to know of no absence of Annabelle Robson from The Clearing at any time. He tried other openings—other ways of finding out what was to him a foregone conclusion. He got no results of any kind whatever.

The same was true of the superintendent. The Ashes had already said that they had never heard the name of Morris in connection with anyone at The Clearing. Whitehouse had still given no sign of life. There was nothing to be gained from staying here. The next day he went to see Robson at his new home near Grantham, on the way from Lincoln to London. It was handsome place, with a magnificent front and huge portico. Just at the moment, two vans were moving some really fine furniture out. Robson was overseeing it.

He nodded to Pointer. "Lucky the price of furniture has gone up, even since we bought. I don't want this sort of stuff now." Pointer waited until Robson led the way into a very barely furnished room. Pointer recalled to him that he was working on the case of a man called Morris, who had been found dead with a paper beside him indicating that it was suicide. This had been the very night of the day on which Mrs. Robson had been murdered. It had since transpired, in the course of the necessary investigation before tomorrow's inquest, the dead man knew Mrs. Robson quite well.

"We know that she came to see him at his office," Pointer said.

"She told me about it," said Robson, "she was near him, and wanted a chat about the Millers. As a matter of fact he knew nothing fresh about them, any more than she did!"

This did not sound like the merry talk of which the office spoke. But Robson, even if not shielding his wife, might well have been given a slightly different version.

Pointer asked if he might look over her rooms. "This Morris affair must be sifted very carefully," he added.

Robson said that he could spend as much time in the house as he liked. He had locked up all his wife's papers in their bedroom. The chief inspector was welcome to go through them, just as Superintendent Clarkson had done, but he himself must leave him as he had things to see to.

Pointer asked him to be kind enough to be on hand when his glance through Mrs. Robson's paper was over. The chief inspector did not expect be more than half an hour at most.

The large bedroom had also been stripped of most of its furniture, but the walls and one corner showed Annabelle's attachment to her native land, of which Whitehouse so often had spoken. All the paintings were of Australian scenes, as was announced on the frames. On the shelves in the corner were some oddments probably from the same source. Shells, some bead necklaces and some old books given, as the inscriptions showed, to Annabelle at Canberra. There were a couple of old Christmas cards, one from "the Miller family." There were very few letters, though those from her home had a drawer to themselves, and her mother's letters were tied with a black ribbon. The cables about her father lay on top. Pointer left the room feeling that the plank on which he had chosen to stand was still too solitary to be built up. Downstairs, he found Robson sitting in front of a sea of papers.

Pointer said that the routine search had not brought to light any link with Morris. "And yet there must have been one, Mr. Robson."

Robson stiffened "I don't get you," he said briefly.

"Why did George Morris kill himself the night after she was murdered? All his affairs were in not merely good but very good condition. He hadn't a care in the world, if we except a possible love affair."

"My wife told me, when I asked her whether he wasn't in a reserved occupation, that he had confided to her that he dreaded being called up. She said he sounded quite worried about it."

"She must have misunderstood him," Pointer replied. "The autopsy proves that his heart really was exceedingly weak. He would never have passed the medical. Yet that note of his about 'the only way out,' does suggest desperation. We think it can only have been caused by some love affair, cannot but link it, as I have just told you, with the death of Mrs. Robson. We think there was a very deep attachment there. Dating back to earlier days, of course. Only on his side, evidently."

There was a pause. Robson's face showed very dark.

"Don't misunderstand me," said Pointer instantly, "I'm not intending to cast the slightest aspersion on Mrs. Robson. But look at Morris' death from our point of view . . . Either he killed himself or he was murdered. There's no possibility—after that note—of his having made some mistake in bottles. No, either suicide or murder. If suicide, then only some unfortunate love affair that went suddenly wrong can explain it. We have gone into his life very thoroughly. There was no girl with who his name was linked, except that faint romance around 'Posey'. No girl in his circle of acquaintance has suddenly married, or been killed, or met with an accident. Except Mrs. Robson. I don't think there's any getting away from that, Mr. Robson. The only possible reason for Morris to have taken poison was the death of your wife on that same morning. He had doubtless lost track of her, and having found her again the shock of hearing of her end must have thrown him off his balance for the time being."

"I think someone at Thoresway who knew what had happened told him. Telephoned probably."

"Who knew Morris?"

"Whitehouse knew him, and any of the others might have known about him. Miss Margaret Ash had seen his name on the parcel, remember."

"I don't care for the idea at all," muttered Robrson.

"Yet it's the only possible explanation of suicide."

"I think you're leaving 'Posey', Miss Miller, too much out of it."

"She could not have stood for anything in his death. There is absolutely nothing known about her by anyone in his circle." Pointer did not intend to be side tracked, and he believed 'Posey'—unless she stood for Mrs. Robson—to be a side issue. "Any attachment with her must have been a very old one—or a very slight one."

"But then—but then," Robson was completely at a loss. "Look here, what are you getting at?" he asked fiercely.

"I'm sorry, Mr. Robson, but of course this death of George Morris, with that letter, leaves me no option."

"Do you mean to say you're going to bring my dead wife's name into that inquest?" Robson leapt to his feet in fury.

"No, no," Pointer said at once. "This is all entirely behind the scenes. The motive for his suicide does not interest the coroner, and it only interests us because we must make certain that his death was suicide, and wasn't murder."

"Whether suicide or murder, the death of that man Morris had nothing to do with my wife, and I strongly resent the idea that it had. I'm afraid I can't spare any more time for ideas. I'm hurrying back to Thoresway as soon as I'm finished here. I haven't finished looking through my cousin's papers yet. And that is urgent."

Pointer had to leave. He had no authority to force the issue, on which, to his way of thinking a great deal depended.

Other efforts to link Morris with Annabelle Robson, or her with him, ended in the same way. The next day's inquest recorded a verdict of *felo de se*. It had to stand, at any rate for the moment.

"I can't see why you think it was murder," said the assistant commissioner. "What's the difficulty in accepting it as suicide?"

"Absolutely no motive, sir, and that bottle beside him, the one that had contained the aconite, had too small a neck to let anyone drink off the contents in a gulp. I've tried it with water. The contents go gurgle-gurgle slowly down your throat, tilt it as you will. And the doctor added that there was a strong smell, not of whisky, or brandy, or gin, alone, but as though the poison had been taken in all three mixed together. Now, there were bottles of all three at Morris' flat, but no glass was left unwashed out of which he could have drunk just before taking poison. Yet, as he never washed up his glasses for himself, why should he have done so before committing suicide? However, sir, I can't waste more time on the case for the present, I see that until Whitehouse is found, I can do no more. He may be able to help me." They turned to other matters.

CHAPTER EIGHT

It was the evening of the day when Pointer had had his talk with Robson at Windhill that the latter returned to Thoresway. He came on Zilla by chance, as she was returning some empty boxes to a cottage near the station. He told her of the talk with the chief inspector. "Scotland Yard seems have a mad idea that this fellow Morris killed himself because of some infatuation with Annabelle. She never met him more than once, or at the outside twice. You never heard her speak of him; did you?"

"Never. Nor has Margaret."

"Yet they even go so far as to think he might have had a hand in Annabelle's death. There's only one explanation of that death"—and Robson outlined a theory very like Tyrwhitt's own. "Say Green saw that, with two murders, he would be rich man, a very, very, rich man. One is over, he has seemed to get away with it. The other is to come, when he thinks it safe. I dropped in at the police station just now to tell the inspector there about it."

"What did he say?" Zilla was listening intently.

"Nothing. Just made notes, quite uninterested one would think. That's the police all over. Yes," he repeated slowly, "if he's not quick, Reg is for it next. What's the matter?" he broke off at something in her face, some pallor.

"Annabelle's death was bad enough, but to think of a devil pretending to be friends with the man he intends to murder next," she said, with a sort of gulp.

"Your saying that you saw a man whom you took to be me, or told me you took to be me"—he looked, at her very straight—"fits in with Green too. A wig on, like my thick mattress, a cap pulled down so as to hold it on well and hide most of it and the face—which would be made up like mine—it could have been Green. . . ."

She nodded without speaking.

"I must get onto their tracks," he said.

"I suppose you'll warn Mr. Whitehouse at once, if you can reach him, about Green?"

"Can't. Or where's the proof that Green murdered Annabelle to come from? We—I and the police, for of course I shall let them in on anything I find out, will have to be on hand to stop him succeeding, but we mustn't stop him trying."

She made some sort of movement.

"I suppose it does sound risky, but it won't be—not with us all watching every move of Green's. It's the only way—he doesn't want me, or I should I him have a go at me with the greatest pleasure."

"Then why did he try to shoot you after killing Annabelle?" she asked.

"I had come in too soon. Don't know what was on foot to which all that disfigurement of Annabelle, after she was dead, points to. But the police think my coming in just then upset some scheme—something which would have let Green out completely, we may be sure. Had he got me, he would have had plenty of hours to carry out any plan of his . . . a plan involving the death of Whitehouse by some apparently natural means, I fancy. He is after big money, all right. Now, all this means that if I too disappear next, don't think I've been done in too. I shall be all right, and shall ring you up, from wherever I am, to tell you how things are going."

"You're on to something!" she said sharply.

"I believe I may be," was his reply, slow as always. "I believe I know where they are," and with that he hurried on, leaving a very disturbed looking Zilla behind him.

What had happened was that at Windhill Robson had come upon Whitehouse's gas mask case which he had left behind after his only visit to the Robson's new home.

In the top of the case was a pocket for papers, and Robson had come on a letter from a Professor Wylie-Houghton. In it the professor spoke of his house Hawkstone at Biddiscombe near Tiverton, of its quiet, and about the way in which he had turned the old stables into workrooms for his experiments. Wylie-Houghton wrote that he would be delighted if Whitehouse would care to come down and try out his own particular theory, a theory in which, frankly, the professor saw some flaws. He himself was often away, and there were no servants living in the house, as only a daily woman came in from time to time. The writer would be distressed to think, should Whitehouse happen to come down, of his finding the place locked against him, so he enclosed a key to one of the side doors which had no inside bolts. He went on to say how pleased he would be to find his friend installed on his return, and begged Whitehouse to use the house without hesitation, and stay a day, a week, or a month, as suited him.

There was no key now in the letter. He hurried on to The Clearing, where was a suitcase full of Whitehouse's papers. This house of Wylie-Houghton's sounded a Godsend to a frightened fugitive, whether alone or with his supposed friend Green.

Robson found the letters at once. They were of no interest except the last, which was dated about a fortnight ago. It told of troubles with the roof, and how Wylie-Houghton had tried in vain to get Dixon, the local builder, to mend it, and put in the bathtub which he had promised months ago.

Robson made a few notes. He then took out his bicycle. He thought hard as he pedaled along. He ran over all Whitehouse's friends and connections and felt certain that, under the circumstances, were he in his cousin's place, he would make for Wylie Houghton's house, and there install himself.

He turned first this, then that, plan over in his mind. Finally he made his choice. The only person he knew who

had ever spoken of Tiverton was Acland. One evening at
the inn bar, it was in the early days of Whitehouse's
arrival, Whitehouse had mentioned having just spent a
day near Tiverton, Acland had at once taken the subject
up, and mentioned that he had been brought up by an
aunt who lived in Tiverton. He knew Hawkstone too, and
mentioned the name of the people from whom Wylie-
Houghton had bought the house. If Acland had been
brought up at Tiverton, he might be most useful now.
Robson intended that he should be. He made for the local
newspaper. Acland seemed very willing to accept an offer
to take a breather at the inn. Robson apologized for his
words on the day of his wife's murder. But as Whitehouse
had his promise, he must still keep to what he said. Only
he should have put it better. "Look here," Robson had
secured a little private parlor, "I want your help just now,
and, in return, offer you the chance of a real newspaper
scoop."

Acland let his light, unfriendly, inquisitive eye flicker
over him. "Go on," he said above the foam of his beer, "go
on."

Robson outlined the police theory of the murder and
its reason, and the probability that it was only the first
step in a double crime. Acland had heard that
Whitehouse was missing, but this idea was new to him

"And you are going to wait to see what happens to
Whitehouse, and so get your proof?" asked Acland.

"Hardly!" said Robson shortly. "An attempt on
Whitehouse's life would be enough—if Green were closely
watched.

"Rather Whitehouse than me!" said Acland to that
"However, where do I come in? You spoke of help, and of
the reward of a scoop?"

Robson went into details of his scheme. In return for
any help that Acland could give him, he would promise to
let Acland have the first news of what he, as well as, the
police, believed might be a really big case. Acland seemed
quite willing. He knew Biddiscombe quite well. Dixon, the

local builder, was a connection of his. He, Acland, could easily get Robson taken on as a worker in need of a holiday, a first-class handy man recovering after pneumonia. Acland was smiling, but his eyes did not smile. They were fixed on Robson's face, still looking him over with their usual unwinking, but very penetrating, stare.

"Where do we leave the police blokes standing?"

"I have to keep in with them, you know," he added.

"I shall let them know."

"When are you going?" asked Acland.

"Tomorrow. Get to London tomorrow night and to Tiverton and Hawkstone by the next after noon."

"Why do I get an impression of you in a green house?" asked Acland suddenly.

"That's clever!" Robson gave him a nod of encouragement. "I'm thinking at this very moment of what flowers I shall cut there to make a wreath for my wife's grave before I go to Devon. Can you often read thoughts?"

"It isn't reading thoughts," Acland said arrogantly, "it goes much deeper than that."

"Does it work with lotteries?" Robson asked him.

Acland gave him one of his coldest looks. "I don't know if you mean that as a joke, but if you mean it seriously—"

"I do!" protested Robson.

"It's not prophetic. Except perhaps where some real calamity threatens, like at The Clearing, or a train that's going to be wrecked."

Early next morning, Robson left Lincoln. He arrived in London in the early afternoon, left his luggage in the cloak room, shaved off his mustache and went to a hairdresser. To him he explained that he had been ordered high frequency treatment by his doctor, and that his hair must be cut as close as possible without being actually shaved. The loss of his mop of curling hair made a great difference in his looks, as he had hoped. By himself, he shaved part of his eyebrows off as well, and then took the Tube to the East End and did some swift shopping, putting his purchases into a suitcase he also bought there, but wearing the terrible old overcoat he had just purchased from a second hand clothes dealer, along with an equally villainous cap. He took a tram towards the station and then a bus. He changed in the cloak room, spent the night in the shelter, and, finally, next morning took his sat in the train, after walking about over a site nearby, where the builders were busy repairing bomb damage. He had a fall near a mound of cement, and, covered with white dust, which got into his hair, turning it a dirty grey, and on to his face, and over his shoes, finally, slouched away. He looked, as he sat humped up in his corner of the train, a builder's assistant of some kind, probably a foreman, with his pencil and steel rule sticking out of his pocket.

Robson was just in time to clamber into the bus which would pass Biddiscombe on its way down to Exeter. Getting out at Biddiscombe, he followed the little map that Acland had drawn for him yesterday. Hawkstone was a yellow brick house, which proved to be as far back from the main road as was The Clearing. It was a big house, and as, smoking a clay pipe, hands in pockets, head down, Robson plodded along the unmade road, he thought over the line that he had decided to take. At first he thought there was no one about; then a man came forward as he made for the back, a man of around his own height, wearing blue sailor's trousers and jersey, with his head bandaged up and a thick black beard. Even Robson, expecting a disguise, could not be sure that it was Green, but he slouched forward to meet the man.

"I'm from Dixon, the builder. About the bath tub. Is the boss—the professor—in?" he asked wheezily.

"I'm a friend of his," said Green's voice. "I'm Mr. Halford—Merchant' Navy." The bronze make-up was excellent, and so was the beard. Robson thought it probable that the bandage helped to hide the ends, and keep it in place. "There are two of us, Mr. Goodwood and myself, staying here. Mr. Wylie-Houghton is away at the moment, but he'll be glad something is going to be done at last about a bathtub. I suppose you know he wants the roof mended first of all?"

"Ah, but we aren't allowed tiles yet awhile," said Robson. "A bath has however just come our way that might do—I'll take all measurements and cart it along this afternoon, if it will do." He stepped towards the back door as he spoke. So far, his own disguise had served him well. He kept his cap over his eyes and his pipe in his mouth as he slouched in to the kitchen. Green led the way up the stairs to the first floor. "As you know, there's one bathroom here, but it's small and inconvenient. This is the room Mr. Wylie-Houghton wrote to your firm about." Green opened a door. Robson stepped in and took his measurements. He was quite at home in this sort of thing. He had helped build the bathroom at The Clearing, which he had put in when it was let to the man who probably was sitting downstairs at the moment, for Green had slipped away, and Robson could hear him talking below. He seemed to have passed muster with Green, but what about Reg? Whitehouse and he were on quite a different footing. No doubts showed on his face however as he opened the door from behind which came the sound of talking—low talking.

"Beg pardon," he said, touching his cap this time, and not looking at a figure in an easy chair. "It's about the damp-proof course here. Mr. Wylie-Houghton still thinks there's something wrong about it. . . ." He went down on his knees, his back to the two men "It's all right, as I told him when he had me up here last time," he said in an aggrieved tone, as he tapped and knocked along the skirting. Rising, he permitted himself to glance at the second figure. He found both men staring hard at, him, but Robson pulled at his pipe, two wards of chewing gum were bulging his cheek nicely. "Back this afternoon," he mumbled, touched his cap again, and walked out with his slow flat-footed gait. Had he possessed a sense of humor he would have found it hard to keep from laughing. Three disguised men! He considered Whitehouse's the least successful. Whitehouse had dyed his hair and now wore a toothbrush mustache, and eyeglasses. His pallor was probably natural under the circumstances. However, Robson now knew that he had not wasted his time. He went to the bus stop, and after a long wait caught the bus back to Tiverton.

The interview with the builder proved to be more difficult. But men were hard to come by, and Acland, in his letter, vouched for Robson's skill with tools. Robson explained that though he was a gardener and handy man, he needed more sheltered work till his lungs got better, which had made him think of combining work with his fortnight's holiday. Wylie-Houghton was one of his best rock-plant customers, said Robson. This surprised Dixon. He himself knew a good deal about that line, and tried a few questions. The answers, satisfied him as to Robson's real knowledge of plants of every kind. He told him to help with a wall that was being repaired at the back of the shop. After watching him for a few minutes at work, Dixon stopped him.

"You'll do. You can have the Houghton job since you want it." They went into the question of wages, and, that settled, Robson next produced to Hawkstone bathroom figures, claiming that Wylie-Houghton had given them to him. Dixon knew all about the bathroom, and he jerked his thumb toward a new tub standing in a shed. Robson next inquired where he could find rooms. Dixon could not help him here, but one of his workmen knew of a woman nearby who might oblige.

It took Robson only a few minutes to arrange with the neat little widow about his room and his food, and then he started off to collect his suitcase and his bicycle. Next he put through a long distance call from the station telephone to Major Findlay. A letter giving all details would be posted tonight, but it might be as well, he thought, to let the police know the whereabouts of the three of them as soon as possible.

As soon as he heard the major at the other end he began: "I hope you recognize the voice? I'm speaking about that cousin of mine by marriage who borrowed your car. His own is a grey Lagonda. I'm speaking from the station telephone at Tiverton. My cousin's down near here with his friend. I'm writing to you by tonight's post."

The chief constable listened in silence till Robson had finished, then he said, "I'm so glad to hear from you, Mr.—eh—I forget the name—Judd? Oh, of course! Well, Mr. Judd, as it happens, my nephew should be down your way tomorrow noon. You'll be on the lookout for him at the Tiverton Station? His train gets in at 4.10. Very good of you to ring me up so promptly and to write to me.

"I appreciate it, I assure you," and with that the talk ended.

Robson wrote a letter telling, in detail, all that had happened. He gave names and addresses, eluding his own, and wound up by stating his uneasiness at the position, and at the same unwillingness to do anything which might prevent a quick ending to the search. Then he went to his uncomfortable bed and slept soundly. Next morning, he was up early and out at Hawkstone by eight o'clock. He brought the milk in and heated up his tin of water for his own tea. He had secured some kippers from his landlady, and the savory smell of one soon floated through the house. Green put his bandaged head over the banister and ask what the devil that smell meant. Judd explained that he always cooked his breakfast on the kitchen stove wherever he worked, that he had wondered whether the professor's friends found it easy to get things, and so had brought along a pair of kippers in case they might come in handy. "Handy!" Green fervently, "look here, if you cook them good as they smell get them ready at once!"

"I'll get yer 'ole breakfast ready, if you like, said Judd obligingly, but hoarsely. "I'm a good cook, I am. Was batman to Colonel Blood, and can cook with anyone."

"Splendid!" came in fervent tones from both men upstairs.

"I'll lay it in the dining room here, and then give you a shout," volunteered Judd.

"Make it so," called Green, in a very quarterdeck voice.

It was the morning before this that Zilla Ash picked up a package addressed to her sister. It was the kind she had seen before, when Whitehouse had occasionally posted his MSS. to Margaret. Flat, not very thick . . . she bent it this way and that. Might easily be a MSS. she decided, and the postmark was—she made it out at last as Biddiscombe or Boddiscombe. The address was printed in a neat hand with an exceedingly fine nib, such a pen as Zilla knew Whitehouse used. She left the parcel on the hall table and looked up the place in an R.A.C. book of hers. There was a Biddiscombe near Tiverton. Zilla let the book drop on the carpet while she reached for the railway guide. Then she sauntered in to the breakfast room and asked for a package of sandwiches to be ready for her as soon as they could be made. She would not be back in for lunch or dinner. Then she went upstairs very noiselessly, threw a few things into a small suitcase which also held her gas mask, and slipped down again to the breakfast roam. Here she found her sandwiches ready, and in a moment was out of the house. She peremptorily stopped the first car—a doctor's—that came her way, and asked for a lift to the station. At the station, she had only a few minutes to spare before the train for London would be in. She did not waste one. Without a glance, or a word of thanks, she streaked out of the car.

She did not trouble about a ticket, but got herself an armful of magazines, and then the best remaining seat in the train. In town she took a taxi to a friend who could always seem to squeeze in one more visitor. Her trust was not misplaced, and next morning she was off for Tiverton by an early train, after telephoning to that station for a car to meet her. At Tiverton, Zilla was slow in getting out of her compartment. She sat well back in her corner, apparently trying to get her suitcase shut again. She did not want to be seen, and so herself was not able to see Tyrwhitt get out of the same train and make for the entrance. There a boy came up to him after watching him loiter about. "You the gent as expected Mr. Judd?" he asked. Tyrwhitt said that he was. "Mr. Judd couldn't leave his job, but he asked me to give you this," and he handed Tyrwhitt an envelope. Tyrwhitt tipped him and, walking on, opened the letter. Robson repeated all the addresses sent to Major Findlay last night, and gave Tyrwhitt directions as to how to get to Hawkstone, where he, Judd, would be waiting for him by the main gate of the house. Failing which, a ring at the back door would bring him down at once.

Zilla meanwhile was well on her way to Biddiscombe by this time. Outside the hamlet, she saw a cottage with *Teas* on a board. She stopped the car, and, going in, ordered whatever passed under that name. While the woman made her a pot, Zilla chatted to her. There was no snobbishness in her make-up. She explained that she was looking for somewhere where she could have a few days' rest from war-work. Where could she get rooms? "Nowhere," was the prompt reply "No one in Biddiscombe has rooms vacant."

"Oh, but that can't be right!" expostulated Zilla, "I know of two men who came down here for a rest only the other day, and they wrote to say how much they liked it here."

"The other day?" queried the woman in tones of utter disbelief. Then she suddenly thought of something. "Ah! The professor's friends, you mean? I did hear Professor Wylie-Houghton has two friends staying there while he's away. Two gents, one of them blown up by a submarine. . . . That would be them?"

"Wylie-Houghton?" asked Zilla, rejoicing. She knew she had heard the name from Margaret as that of a friend of Whitehouse's engaged on much the same line of work. Zilla made an exceedingly good tea, paid off the taxi, and then walked on to Hawkstone. Inside, standing well in the shade of the shrubs, she studied the house carefully. She had no idea of how she was going to proceed. Zilla never made plans. She saw a workman, a plumber or a builder, apparently, pass to and fro on the upper story. He seemed to be waiting for something, as half the time his head was out of window scanning the road. Zilla had slipped in the second and smaller gate, out of his ranged view, and now, when he had turned away, moved around to the front where he could not see her.

The windows of one of the downstairs room were open. Outside the windows, not far from them, and facing their way, was a summerhouse on the lawn. From the summerhouse smoke was curling up, and Zilla could see, as she moved to one side, a panama hat showing through the very open back. That would be Whitehouse. A moment later, a bandaged, bearded figure stepped through the window, and came across to the white hat. Was this Robson? Then her sense told her that it must be Green. As for the workman on the floor above, she took him for the genuine article.

She waited where she was for a minute longer, then the two men, Green and Whitehouse, as she now guessed they must be, went into the house. together, through the long windows. A short time later, the bandaged figure in navy blue walked down to the path, and out the main gate, making for a corner where the bus for Exeter passed. In a moment Zilla was through the windows, into the room. She was there nearly ten minutes. Coming out, she was making her way carefully, as before, to the gate by which she had entered, when a sound from the road made her stop. A horse was coming along, a horse and cart. It stopped at the gate by which she had come in. She walked on and saw a cart laden with firewood. Standing at the back was a man, busy arranging his logs. "Any wud, Miss?" he asked in a thick, Devonshire voice. As he turned, he showed as a thin gipsy-looking fellow, with long black hair and face, smudged with charcoal, brown as a berry. And black with what looked like two days growth of hair.

"Ask at the house," was her reply. This could not be Robson anyway, he was too tall. Taking some wood under each arm, he passed her, whistling between his teeth, his head turned from her.

At the back door he gave a knock that could have been heard all over the house. Judd came down.

"Na then, 'oo're you?" he demanded.

"Wud," said the gipsy-looking man. "I'm wud." Followed a sentence in a rich Devonshire burr, the man pushing his way into the house as he spoke. Finally Judd understood that the woodman had an unpaid account which he wanted settled. Judd called out; "Someone wants a word with the professor," and watched the man's progress. At the living room door he listened a moment, knocked and went in without waiting for an answer. The man standing at the table wheeled with an exclamtion, and then stood still, staring at the newcomer in apparent terror.

Again came a long sentence in what was broad Devonshire, but which to the other man might well have been some Eastern tongue. At last Whitehouse made out that the grubby bit of paper, with the grimy numbers on it, which the man fish from a tattered pocket, was an account, meant for the absent professor.

Came another sentence. The man was evidently trying to speak with less of his native burr. At last he made it clear that he came daily to look after the stock of wood in the house, and to see to it that there was always plenty either of logs or of kindling. He would split enough of the latter if need be.

Whitehouse now, bent over his papers in an obvious hurry to get rid of him. But at last he went, and the writer listened intently to his very loud footsteps. When he heard the back door slam, Whitehouse, mopped his forehead, and sank back in the chair. At the gate the man passed Ziila pressed close into some evergreen bushes.

"Hey, you!" she called softly, as the man clambered into his seat, and swung herself up beside him. "Ten shillings to take me into Tiverton," she held the note out as she spoke.

The man started to argue, but Zilla would have none of it. After a second he yielded, flicked the reins, and drove off. A man was coming along the road to their left. Zilla had a handkerchief over her head. She pulled it well forward, and sat low in her seat, In another moment she and the cart were around the bend.

Tyrwhitt stopped at the gate, and pushed it carefully open. His first reaction, as Judd came forward, touching his cap, was to burst out laughing. Then he followed him to the kitchen.

"I don't suppose there's any risk to be expected at this moment?" he asked

"Green's gone to Exeter."

"Right. Then we'll talk all this out. I'll make for that cupboard if I hear steps. I must say your disguise is first rate.

"Has to be," said Judd. "Whitehouse and I know each other too well to be careless, and he's a very scared man. It's as you thought. Green poses as his preserver. Whitehouse can't bear to let him out of his sight. But Green was very firm about having to go to Exeter today and get some stores in. I heard him telling Reg only this morning that while he was around nothing could happen to him. Whitehouse doesn't intend to set foot outside the gates. So far, they accept me without question as Dixon's workman."

"I don't wonder. By the way, how many gates are there? I only saw two. The main one, and a second to the right of it."

"Those are the only ones. The main gate seems to be the only one in much use. It's nearer to the bus stop."

They now went into careful details. Tyrwhitt thought it would be best to stay in Hawkstone itself and take on the night watching. The local police, as well as the Exeter police, had been notified to stand ready for an emergency call.

"I suppose you can stow me away somewhere?" asked Tyrwhitt.

"Easy," Robson assured him. "The two men only use a sitting room and the dining room and their bedrooms. I shall be very glad to have you here," Robson said, when it was settled.

"I don't think we shall have long to wait"—Robson gave it as his opinion. "It seems to me Green must want to get it over with, and be able to live an ordinary life once more."

"So he thinks!" put in Tyrwhitt.

"How do you expect the—incident—to happen?" Robson asked him.

"An accident—any time. And then Green would pose as being on hand merely to help a friend, who was a nervous wreck. He, Green, being sure of the friend's innocence . . . that will be his line, we fancy. After which, we expect an attempt to fit the murder at The Clearing on to the dead Whitehouse." Tyrwhitt was turning out his suitcase as he spoke. He had brought food with him, and a camera, and various other things that might be needed, including an automatic, and a police whistle. Robson, or rather Judd, helped him stow the food away, and then made him a sign to follow. They tiptoed up the black stairs, which were of stone, to a room on the other side of the landing from the rooms of Whitehouse and Green, but which gave a view of their doors. It was the housekeeper's room, and close to the passage off which the bathroom opened where Judd was putting in the new tub. Meantime, he was acting as the houseman, and in that character, was constantly on hand by day.

CHAPTER NINE

Tyrwhitt's room at Hawkstone had the great merit of being over the unused, locked-up drawing room at the other end of the house from that used by the two men downstairs, so that he could move about with freedom. Robson's hours were from eight in the morning till five at night, though he had explained to the two men that, provided he was paid overtime, he had no objection to staying until nine o'clock. They had accepted gladly. The daily woman had long since taken to munition work. Neither of them could cook, and Robson was quite good in that line. He explained to Tyrwhitt that he went into the living room as little as possible, which suited them as well as it did him. For the same reason, he added, he would lay the table, and bring in the meal, leaving the food on a tray on the sideboard, and give a shout of "Everything's ready," after which he would busy himself in the kitchen until he heard them leave the dining room and go into the living room opposite. There was a gas fire and a gas ring in the room. Robson had brought up from below a kettle, a saucepan, some tinned soups and meat, some simple cutlery and cup. He added a loaf of bread, and a pot of marmalade, and had seen to it that there were plenty of books. Tyrwhitt declared that he would be in clover.

"You seem to expect that I shall be here by this month." Robson said that it might be some time before Green would take the last step in his program. Tyrwhitt did not agree "He can't be sure that Wylie-Houghton won't come back unexpectedly"—as you did at The Clearing, he nearly added. They tried out the door ajar, and Robson found that, if necessary, it could be left so and yet look closed. On which, Robson went on with his

work in the bathroom. Tyrwhitt listened attentively to his
quick, but heavy tread. Tyrwhitt had arranged with Judd
that, whenever possible, Judd would slip a note under the
door if he had to leave the house on any lengthy errand.

Nothing happened during the remainder of the day,
nor during the night. In the morning he mentally ticked
off the happenings in the house by the time table that
Judd had given him. The breakfast shout rang out at
nine, to the minute as expected. Two hours passed. He
heard Judd come upstairs and tidy the two men's
bedrooms, then get to work carpentering in the bathroom.
Tyrwhitt dozed off. At eleven he heard Green let himself
out of the front door. He came back very shortly, having
just stepped out for a newspaper. Then Judd slipped a
note under his door to tell him that he had been sent on
an errand to a certain tobacconist in the village. Tyrwhitt
set his door ajar. Five minutes passed. Another five went
by. Then suddenly, terribly, came a long, wild screech,
high pitched, ending in a dreadful, but short, gurgle. It
seemed to come from outside the house. Tyrwhitt was
down the stairs in a couple of jumps, and out of the door.
There was nothing to be seen. Running round the house
he saw Green, with his back to him, holding something in
his right hand, bending over a white, panama-hatted
figure in the summerhouse. Blood was dripping from
what he held. There was blood on the crown of the
panama hat. Tyrwhitt could not afford to take a chance.
He brought the butt end of his automatic down on Green's
head. Green promptly slumped down to the ground. One
glance at the figure in the summerhouse was enough to
tell the Army man that it was a dead man and also that it
was not Whitehouse, was not anyone whom Tyrwhitt
thought that he had ever seen before. The sitting room
glass doors were standing open. Tyrwhitt dragged Green
in, and tied him up with cords from the two curtains.
Then he put through a code call to the police. A police
Officer was to come at once, and bring the police
ambulance. Someone had been killed at Hawkstone.

"I'll come at once myself, with a constable," said the sergeant who took the call. Tyrwhitt shouted for Whitehouse. No one replied. He searched the house hastily. It was quite empty. He ran to the gate and waited. In a very short time two bicycles ridden by a stout constable and still stouter sergeant turned the bend. Tyrwhitt swung the gate open. He took them to the summerhouse, where one stood on guard while the other, the constable followed him inside to where Green lay, unconscious and trussed up. Tyrwhitt ran upstairs for his camera, and photographed the dead man in the summerhouse from every possible angle

"Who is he?" asked the sergeant "I've never seen him before. Have you, Joe?"

Joe called back that he had seen the man once before, but without the panama hat on. It was this very morning, when he had passed the police station driving a cart with some logs in it in this direction. The sergeant and Tyrwhitt were both bending very low over the man. Both gave an exclamation at the same time.

"That's a wig!"—"And those lines around his eyes are painted. But we can't touch him till the super arrives," added the sergeant. A call from Joe in the sitting room told that Green was stirring.

"Let him be," said the sereant, "we don't want his evidence yet awhile. Not till the super arrives,"

Tyrwhitt inferred that, strictly speaking, the murder itself should have waited till the super arrived. He went into the living room to telephone to the village in order to get in touch with Robson at the tobacconist's.

"Come back at once, you're urgently needed, was Tyrwhitt's message. He hung up before Robson could ask any questions, and took up his post by the dead man. Who was he? Was his death a mistake? Was it possible that Green had had accomplice, who had followed him down here? Was it Green and not Whitehouse, who was on the run? Not long after the front gate clanged shut.

Tyrwhitt shouted, and Robson came hurrying around the bend.

"What's wrong? Oh, Good God! So he got him!" And Robson bent over the figure with the stained and broken white hat. Then he stared at Tyrwhitt, then he stared again at the dead man.

"What's this mean? Who is—why it's the woodman!"

Tyrwhitt told him of the struggle with Green. "As for the rest—the explanation of who this is I know no more than you."

"Then where's Reg? Where's Whitehouse? Did he get him too?" Robson was staring back into the sitting room beyond where the massive man in blue was busy with Green, who was half trying to rise, half trying to roll off the couch. "Can't find him. The sergeant is hunting the house for him."

Robson was into the house on the run. Tyrwhitt stayed with the body. They found no trace of Whitehouse, but signs that he had taken several small things with him, enough to fill a travelling bag. They had just finished their search, when a car could be heard driving up fast and well. It was followed by an ambulance. The car was full of police. One was the superintendent from Exeter, a tall saturnine-faced man who spoke very little, but who set things stirring with a speed that made Tyrwhitt realize how it came that his subordinates could afford to wait for his arrival. While one of the constables was taking photographs of the dead man, Superintendent Hood examined the summerhouse very closely from the outside. It was a very thin wooden structure, quite pretty now in summer, when the climbing roses were out, but very rickety and dilapidated under its decoration. They could see the place where the murderer had struck from behind, through the light trellis work. Four teak chairs, and a very firm teak table was all the furniture.

"Where are Whitehouse's papers?" Nothing whatever lay on the table. "And where is he? Have you searched the gardens?" asked Robson of Tyrwhitt, who shook his head.

The police were doing that, and doing it thoroughly. The superintendent made for the telephone, and sent out instructions to detain anyone answering to Whitehouse's description who could not prove his identity. He added that White house was not to be arrested. He was merely wanted very urgently as a most material witness in a very important case. That done, and after looking Green carefully over, he returned to the summerhouse and stared about him. No footprints were possible in the dry, well-firmed gravel paths. The bloodstained axe, which Tyrwhitt had wrested from Green was standing where he had placed it, leaning against one of the chairs just inside the summerhouse. The superintendent stood listening for a moment. "What's the water running" he asked. Searching, they found a small garden tap running.

"Turned on to wash his hands?" asked Robson. But Tyrwhitt said that as he had caught Green literally red-handed, the tap had probably been turned on to prevent any cry of the victim being heard. "Though nothing could have drowned the screech I heard."

Once the official photographs of the dead man were taken, he was laid on the kitchen floor, and Superintendent Hood lifted off the panama hat, or what remained of it, laid it carefully aside, and began to wash the dead face. Tyrwhitt and Robson watched with breathless interest. "I've seen that face before!" said Tyrwhitt, "connected with this case, too. Ah!" The superintendent pulled the hair firmly by its center locks. The wig came away in his hand leaving a head covered with thin, straight, light brown hair that clung damply to the contours.

"Why! It's Acland!" Robson almost shouted.

"Acland? Acland?" queried Tyrwhitt. "I place him now!"

Robson was staring at the man's boots and legs. "He was the woodman who called yesterday morning. And to think I never recognized him! What on earth does this mean? Why was he wearing Whitehouse's panama—and in the summerhouse?"

The superintendent asked Robson his account of the happenings of the morning.

"Around ten, Whitehouse had taken his writing out to the summerhouse and said that he intended to work there til lunch. Robson said that he heard him tell Green not to disturb him. The overhanging roof of the summerhouse prevented anyone on the top floor from seeing inside it. Green had left the house about an hour later, to slip down to the village. A little later, Robson could not be sure of the time, he returned, and a few minutes after that Whitehouse had called Robson to get him some tobacco from the village.

"Did you see his face?" asked the superintendent.

"No, he was sitting too far inside the summerhouse."

"Are you sure it was he who spoke?"

"Oh, yes. It was Whitehouse all right."

"Yet Green was misled as to who was in the summerhouse," Tyrwhitt reminded him.

"Gosh, yes!" Robson was silent a moment on that.

"I went at once after slipping you a note," he turned to Tyrwhitt, "and, thinking there was no rush, I delayed a bit, trying to buy a lighter. Some new ones have just come in. Then the telephone rang, and I rushed back here."

Tyrwhitt had taken the time when Green left the house. It had been eleven. He had returned at eleven eighteen. At eleven twenty-five, Robson had passed him the note, and then had left the house for the village and the tobacconist's. At quarter to twelve had come the terrible scream from the garden, which had brought him—Tyrwhitt—running out of his room. He had looked at the watch lying beside him as he leaped to his feet. A quarter to twelve could therefore be taken as moment of the murder,

"The amazing riddle is how, and why, Acland, came into this," continued Tyrwhitt.

Robson cleared up one end of it. He had needed Acland to help him get quickly into Hawkstone in some plausible, vouched-for shape. But as to why Acland had come on down in disguise, why he had apparently wished to be mistaken for Whitehouse in the summerhouse, Robson said he could not even hazard a guess. He told of Acland's coming into the house the day before as the woodman, and of the talk he had with Whitehouse, and possibly Green. Not taking him for anything but what he seemed, Robson said that he had not tried to hear what was said. Yet now, thinking back, he thought that Whitehouse had looked rather odd that evening, and had not talked at all to Green. "I rather think now, that Whitehouse was beginning to have his suspicions of Green. Certainly he was very short with him, very silent, and went to bed quite early."

"It looks as though Acland were mixed up more deeply than we can understand at present," said Tyrwhitt. Robson said that he had not seen Acland, as the woodman, that morning at all; evidently he had used the second gate. "I only know it was Whitehouse who was in the summerhouse when I went for the tobacco."

"Could the chap imitate Whitehouse's voice, do you think?" persisted the superintendent.

Robson looked a little uncertain.

The body was lifted into the ambulance. Green went in the ambulance too. He had come around, but was in no condition to be questioned. Tyrwhitt and Robson were each asked to come down to the police station and sign their statements, after which they would be free to leave. Meantime, the country was being scoured for Whitehouse.

Robson said he could imagine his feelings when he read of the murder of Acland, evidently in his stead.

"Looks as if Reg had realized his danger at the last moment, and just got away in time."

Tyrwhitt thought it looked a good deal more complicated than that, but he said nothing.

"And I was not there" said Robson, "I'm just as well have stayed at home, and got on with my own affairs!"

"It rather looks," said Tyrwhitt, "as though your cousin sent you to the village to get you out of the way. He thought of you as Judd, remember. I think he must have got out of the house, then, when you were away. Well, the police down here will take over now, together with Superintendent Clarkson who, so my uncle has just telephone me, will be lent them for a few days."

Tyrwhitt and Robson traveled up together to London and then on the next day to Lincoln. The talk inevitably turned on the only thing that could occupy Robson's mind at the moment, that was the murder of his wife.

Next day, at Lincoln station, Major Findlay was waiting for his nephew. Robson excused himself from accepting the major's offer of a lift, wanted to get to The Clearing as quickly as possible.

"I think you will alter your mind about not coming with us, when you see what I've got in the back of the car," said Findlay, speaking with confidence. Tyrwhitt took it that Zilla Ash was there, so did Robson. As soon, however, as he caught sight of the man looking expectantly out of the window, he gave a leap forward, and wrung Whitehouse's hand with very evident relief and pleasure. Tyrwhitt followed suit.

"How did you do it, Reg?" asked Robson, relief in his voice.

"Good going," said Tyrwhitt "By the way, may I introduce you to the gent as put in your bath at Hawkstone," he waved a hand at Robson.

"Not finished," said Robson. "Too much waiting at table for that!"

They all laughed at the stupefaction on Whitehouse's face.

"Well, Robson, changed your mind about coming along?" asked the Major. "There's room."

"You bet!" said Robson fervently.

By common consent they did not discuss the events foremost in their minds till they got to the chief constable's house, and were seated in his library. Then Findlay became chairman, as it were.

"First of all, I'll tell you what I've heard this morning from Exeter. Green has now recovered. I suggest, Geoff, that, from the point of view of not delaying an investigation, you give a lighter tap in future. However, as I say, he has been questioned, and this is his story. You mustn't mind the way he speaks of you, Mr. Whitehouse The chief constable unfolded a report which had just arrived by post. His story is that it's all a put-up job, of which he's the innocent victim.

"Whitehouse has done him brown. When he seemed to lose his nerve completely after Mrs. Robson's murder, he, Green, had nobly stood by a friend, who was, he had then thought, innocent. They had not been together, the day of the murder. Both had said at breakfast that they were going to Lincoln, and Whitehouse had had his car out. Green had gone by train. As arranged, Whitehouse and he had met for tea, and driven home together .On the way into Thoresway, they had met the postman and Whitehouse had heard of the murder. When they drove on, Whitehouse had been very frightened. He had actually been in to The Clearing, to get the A.B.C. now in the car, he said, around, or just before, the time the murder had been done. Supposing he had been seen going in or coming out? Green, sorry for him, had at once suggested that they should claim to have spent the whole day together in Lincoln. They had gone over their story very carefully, but, when questioned down at the police, station, apparently Whitehouse had contradicted himself rather badly. At least so he said—"

"I'll say it too," threw in Findlay, glancing at Whitehouse for a second rather grimly, before he read on.

"It was Whitehouse who had suggested the getaway in his car that night. Green had let himself be persuaded, partly from good nature, partly because of the very high sum Whitehouse had offered him. It was Green who had left the garage door ajar with the light on, who had knocked out Tyrwhitt, and bundled him into Whitehouse's car, as he had thought the police car would, or might, have more petrol. This had turned out to be the case, and the two, Whitehouse and Green, had driven to London. Whitehouse had been in to his bank in the late afternoon, had drawn out everything standing to his credit, and taken his Bearer shares away with him.

"They had got to London in ample time to catch the early morning train to Tiverton and to a house which Whitehouse had chosen. All this time, Green swore, he had believed he was only running away with a frightened, but innocent man. He felt sure, he said, that in a short time the police would get on the real murderer's track, and that then he and Whitehouse could return. The idea that Whitehouse was planning anything so diabolical as another murder, so arranged that it would be pinned on him, Green said, had never entered his head. Apparently he had no idea of who the murdered man really was. Green went on to say that both realized that they must disguise themselves, as their pictures or descriptions were sure to be given to the police. They took the names of Goodwood and Halford; and went out as little as possible. A builder's man from a local firm turned out to be willing and able to do their simple housekeeping. The man who was murdered brought wood the day after their arrival, and said he was paid by Wylie-Houghton to see that his supply was kept up to the limit. As for yesterday—Green said that Whitehouse had been in a curious mood the day before. Silent and apparently absorbed in thought.

He, Green, had gone out to the village for a paper at eleven, come back and had a glass of whiskey and soda in the sitting room, saw what he took to be Whitehouse with his panama on, still sitting where he had left him, working in the summerhouse and had begun to read the paper, his back to the open window. Then had come that dreadful screech, he had dashed out to Whitehouse, found a bloodstained wood chopper lying across the entrance to the summerhouse, and Whitehouse, as he thought, slumped down in his chair dead. Green had automatically picked up the axe as he rushed in, suddenly thought it did not look like Whitehouse, in spite of the panama hat, and was bending down to make sure, when he had, himself, been struck down—by the murderer, he had first thought."

The major replaced the sheets carefully. Then he turned to Whitehouse. "And now for your story in detail."

Whitehouse flushed deeply. He pressed his thin, nervous lips together for a moment, and then he nodded. "Right. Where shall I start?"

"Start from the beginning."

"Well, the day Annabelle—died—I spent the morning in the car in the woods nearby. It was a glorious day, you may remember, and I am fond of working out of doors in a car. Then I needed a book I had meant to tell Green to buy in Lincoln. He had gone in after breakfast, and, as he says, I was to pick him up at tea around half past four at the White Hart. But I didn't want to drive to Lincoln, as petrol was a bit low. And as I wasn't sure of the next train in, it was then around one o'clock, and as I was near The Clearing, I went in and took the A.B.C. back to the car. Yes," he looked at the startled expressions around him, "I must have been in the house just before the actual moment. The sitting room was empty, but I heard Annabelle at the boiler stove. I didn't want to be delayed so I just took the book from its place in the corner without speaking, and stepped out again. I saw that I had better go by car, so I dropped the railway guide in the back, and drove off to Lincoln. The rest is as Green says. On the way back, the postman met us and told us of the dreadful news.

"At first no thought of any suspicion lighting on me occurred to me. It was Green who very kindly pointed that out, and more than pointed it out, harped on it, rubbed it in. I began to realize what it meant; that I had no alibi. He offered at once to say that we had been together all the day, and I was very glad to agree. It never occurred to me—then—to notice that the various places where he claimed to have been were all very vague. He hadn't lunched anywhere he said, but had had a couple of beers at The Saracen's Head. Well, he often did just that. There was nothing to arouse any suspicions, I want to assure you most solemnly of that," Whitehouse looked anxiously around him.

"Your later conduct rather bears out your trust in him," said Findlay with a faint grin.

"I was too rattled, too horrified, too overcome at what had happened to give a very coherent account of myself to you police, I'm afraid. That afternoon, knowing how I had blundered, and contradicted myself at the police station, believing that I would be arrested first thing in the morning, I went to my bank and drew out all my available balance and some of my securities. Then I told Green what I had done, and that I intended to get away that night to Hawkstone. I told him all about where that was and said that if the Professor should be there, so much the better. He would shelter me—I mean—" Whitehouse caught himself up. "I mean, I felt sure I could convince him of my innocence." He hurried on. "Green offered to come with me. He absolutely refused to leave me in the state in which I was. I was very grateful to him. It was he who was certain that the inn would be watched, but said that he would leave everything in its place so as to look as though he were coming back, get out of his room by the stackpipe, put a ladder against my window, and get the car out. I was to take everything I needed and we would be off. There would be a watch outside as well as inside, he thought, but he said he had a plan for dealing with that."

"He had. Quite a good one." Tyrwhitt assured him gravely.

"Well, all went as we planned. We altered our appearance sitting in the back of the car; Green had prepared for that. We caught a train for Tiverton the next morning. The car was left in a garage near the station.

"At Hawkstone, Green and I made ourselves comfortable and hoped for the best. Food was not going to be difficult we found, for Wylie-Houghton had laid in a quantity of tins. Green went into the village, and explained us as friends of Wylie-Houghton, and arranged for bread to be sent out. Milk, Wylie-Houghton had forgotten to countermand, and we found bottles of it in the scullery. We were horrified by the arrival of a man from the Tiverton builder to put in a bathtub. I never thought of you, Harold, I must say I didn't like it at first, but as you really seemed to know your job, I began to think you might be very useful—"

"When did you first begin to suspect Green?" asked Findlay.

Whitehouse fell into a sort of reverie. "I was never fond of him," he said at last "But I thought him the usual type. Out for his own interests, but not a shark. However, down at Hawkstone—I seemed to see him in a different light . . . began to see that I had put myself very thoroughly in his power. I decided that I would get away when the woodman came. The woodman—of whom I know absolutely nothing by the way—came, as he had done the day before to chop up kindling. He said that he had an arrangement with Wylie-Hought to do that—"

"Professor Wylie-Houghton's absence seems to have suited quite a number of people," said Findlay. "But go on."

"I had packed some of my things, and slipped out—"

"One moment, where were you sitting?"

"In the summerhouse, with my bag under the seat. By the way, just before the man was due, I set Judd, as he was to me, off to the village. I hoped to do just what I did do, get away, in the woodman's cart. Though had I any idea of what I was leaving him to—" Whitehouse turned very pale. "I went to him in the outhouse where he was chopping wood, and offered him a hundred pounds for the hire of his cart for the rest of the day. He stared thoughtfully at the ground—he never once met my eye. I was afraid he was going to refuse, in which case I was going to ask him to drive me to some nearby station . . . but after a moment he said 'Right. Done along of you,' or some such words. He spoke a very broad Devonshire. He wrote down an address on a tag, as that of his shop at Tiverton, which I was to tie to the cart and hand it over, to any inn, or pub, who would look after the horse and cart till he would fetch it. I left him in the shed. Went out by the second gate, where the cart was. Waited there till you, Harold, at last went down the village. And then I drove off down a side lane. I felt very nervous, and stopped for a moment to tie a cloth I found in the back over my head and under my chin; the horse blanked I put around my shoulders, and, looking, I hoped like an old market woman I drove off. I couldn't bear to get out of my rug and face a train, so I jogged on through the night, till a car nearly ran me down. The man driving helped me get the thing to the grass where he tethered the horse. I tied the label on, and then, hearing he was going to London insisted on his taking me there. He was half amused at my cheek—and at my clothes. I told him I had toothache and huddled up in them til we reached London. There I left him, and got paper and—well—you can imagine my feelings. I telephoned you, Major, that I would be here by the first train possible. I came—and here I stay, for the present."

Robson said that he hoped Whitehouse would come with him and stay at his new home. Whitehouse agreed with pleasure. The police also like the arrangement, for it would keep two most important witnesses on hand together.

"Where did you leave your panama hat, Mr. Whitehouse?" asked the chief constable.

"In the summerhouse, I suppose. Let me think,"— Whitehouse did so—"yes, on one of the chairs in the summerhouse. Where evidently that poor chap found it, and put it on to keep the sun from his eyes. Is it of any importance—I mean where I left my hat. Why do you ask?"

"It was put on the dead man *after* he was killed," said Findlay, and got the sensation he expected "There is no doubt about it," he continued, "for one thing, the cut in it is not long enough for the injury to the head supposed to have been inside it. Acland was killed by a terrific blow struck with the wood chopper, and then the hat was slashed with a knife, or cut with scissors, and stuck on the head."

"I left my paper shears behind me," said Whitehouse. "I gathered my papers into the suitcase, but forgot the scissors."

"They were found thrown down under one of the chairs in the garden house. But the point that the man, Acland, was not wearing your hat, seems to rule out the first idea that a mistake in identity had been made."

"I'm very glad to hear it!" said 'Whitehouse.

"By Jove, uncle, Green is a lightning worker," said Tyrwhitt, "he hadn't much time before I was on the spot."

"Then Green knew it was Acland," murmured Whitehouse. "He had recognized him in his disguise as a woodman, you think?"

"Or did he intend to pass him off as you—dressed up in your clothes?" suggested Robson. "Is this another interrupted crime? You see, Green didn't know about Tyrwhitt being in the house. He would think he had it all to himself."

"But what about me,?" asked Whitehouse promptly. "If he intended to pass off Acland as me—what about me later on?"

"Done in too," said Robson to that—"later on."

"That's a possibility," agreed Findlay, "we believe it's just possible that some elaborate plan was started when he murdered your wife. This may have been another. We think that he and Acland—whom evidently he had recognized in spite of his disguise—were old acquaintances. It would account for Acland being in the summerhouse, supposing he had arranged with Green to meet him there. Acland had been mixed up with people suspected of being blackmailers," said Findlay, "how closely we don't know yet."

"I can't think he had recognized Acland," said Whitehouse suddenly. "I really can't! He seemed so genuinely indifferent to the man. I heard them talking the day before, when Green couldn't have known. I overheard him. It was the unmistakable idle talk of a bored man having a word with workman on the place."

"He never talked to me," said Robson.

"No, because you were making such a noise breaking into the wall that one couldn't hear oneself speak. But as I say, I heard every word Green said to Acland the morning before—and he certainly didn't know who he was then."

"I wonder if Acland read his thoughts," said Robson suddenly. "On the day when I talked with him about my going to Hawkstone in disguise, he read my mind quite out of the blue. I was thinking of cutting some special flowers for Annabelle's grave. Well, if he could do that, when the thoughts were only unimportant ones, isn't it possible that yesterday morning he got some glimpse of Green's thoughts about you, Reg, and showed it?"

"Knowing what we do, I think Acland was in half a mind to refuse me the cart. I wish he had, for I should then have suggested our driving off in it together. He seemed jerky, and on edge. He jumped when I came into the shed, I now remember. He was using that very axe and he almost dropped it as I spoke to him from behind."

"He must have come down with some definite purpose in view," said Findlay. "Blackmailing a murderer must be a very touch-and-go business."

"In more senses than one," murmured his nephew.

"On the whole," said Findlay, "I think that will be the police line. Acland suspected Green of being the murderer."

"Then his words, when he held the button, about seeing two women in Mrs. Robson's murder was just acting?" said Tyrwhitt.

"Naturally!" said his uncle. "Acland suspecting, shall we say, the truth, goes down to Hawkstone in order to blackmail Green. It certainly looks as though one of them must have given the other an appointment. Green to go to the summerhouse, or Acland to go into the house. From the fact that he seemed to you, Mr. Whitehouse, as being worried or, at least, on edge, it looks as though he had decided to speak to Green as soon as possible. In that case, it's just possible that, until he spoke, Green had not recognized him, in that case the murder would have been in swift retaliation."

Robson rose. He was looking forward to seeing Zilla and telling her that he had redeemed his promise of finding his wife's murderer.

"No other news about any of the people here?" said Whitehouse, apparently speaking idly.

"None, except that Miss Ash has joined the A.T.S."

"What?" asked Robson in amazement, "when?"

"This morning. She telephoned her people from London that she had just joined up a couple of hours before your train got here."

"But her work? Surely it was a reserved occupation?" said Whitehouse, as Robson seemed too surprised to say anything more.

"It is. But a little thing like that wouldn't stop Miss Ash. She's an A-1 driver, Clarkson always says, and they're badly needed in the Army. She pulled some War Office strings, and the A.T.S. took her at once."

"Is this official?" asked Robson in a dazed voice.

"It is. When Miss Margaret Ash told us about her sister's message, we got on to the London Recruiting Office at once, and they confirmed it."

CHAPTER TEN

Robson went to Ing's Place at once. Mrs. Ash was very gracious. She even pressed him to stay to dinner, but Robson excused himself. There was too much for him to see to he told her, and then went on to say how surprised he had been by the news about Zilla.

Mrs. Ash hesitated. She liked Robson, and felt that the family owed him much for the way in which he had kept his head in the days when her daughter seemed to have lost hers.

She said simply: "You don't mind if I'm frank, do you—Harold? I know about her infatuation for you, she told me about it, and that she hoped to marry you, in the future, when this tragic affair should be a thing of the past. Well, you know Zilla, Harold. It's always *Fata Morgana* that attracts her. The thing she couldn't have was the one thing she wanted, even as a baby. When she could have it, or got it, it lost all charm, and was dropped for something else in the distance. I talked with her on the telephone today as you know. It's happened again— with you—that's all. She was very sorry about it, but quite definite."

"But"—began Robson, then stopped.

"Forgive me, if I say it can't be a real blow," went on the mother. "I don't think Zilla is the type that should marry, but, if she does, it should be a man much older than herself, who will understand her temperament, and make allowances."

"But I thought—she told me—" He bit his lips.

"That she loved you," finished Mrs. Ash. "Zilla, as yet, is incapable of love, Harold. Life may teach it to her, but so far, all she can feel is passion, and glamour, and the liking to let herself go; and the hope that she may be swept away on the wave of some romantic emotion."

"But I can't let it end like this!" he protested. " I can't let it rest here."

"She wants it to," said the mother firmly. "Why not have a talk with her on the telephone? That will convince you that there's nothing to be done."

"May I?" said Robson. He got her very quickly.

"Harold?" she said, in a very businesslike tone. "Oh, yes, Harold. Well, darling, I suppose Mother has told you about me? Then you know that I made a mistake when I thought—well, what I thought. I don't feel like that any more, and when that happens, I know, from experience, that it's no use waiting for the feeling to come back. It's dead as a dead flower. Sorry, but that's how it is."

"But why did you join the Army? When can I see you? I've such a lot to tell you, I thought you'd be thrilled to know that Green is under lock and key. You seemed so anxious to help."

"I was," she threw in casually, "but that's gone too. Now I'm only keen on Army life, and I know it's going to suit me as nothing else ever has. Forget me, Harold, or, think of me as a very silly idiot who didn't know what was real, from what wasn't."

"But you'll be wanted at the trial," he said to that. "It was your coat, remember! And what about the man you saw at the window?"

"I don't know what you're talking about," said Zilla, very firmly. "I must have been pulling your leg. I didn't see anyone at the window. I couldn't, as I wasn't there to see him. And as to the coat that I threw away—I'll send in my evidence about that, from wherever I am stationed."

"It will have to be sworn to," he said a trifle grimly.

"It will be," she replied lightly. "But count me out, Harold. I've taken the modern equivalent of the veil. My hair has been cropped already, and I'm just about to be handed a scrubbing brush and a bar of kitchen soap. Good-bye," and with that, she hung up.

Robson went back to Mrs. Ash. "You're right," he said. "As far as Zilla is concerned, I'm something the cat brought in last year."

She made a sympathetic noise, and was: genuinely sorry for him, but as genuinely relieved at the turn events had taken.

Margaret arrived on a short visit soon after Robson had left. A hospital car, fetching operation instruments from the station, put her down, and would take her back. Her feelings when she had read in the papers about the events at Hawkstone, had been of amazement, pure and simple.

"I never liked Mr. Green, but to murder first Annabelle and then Mr. Acland!"

"Mr. Robson has been in. He's very thankful that Annabelle's murderer has been caught so quickly. We talked of Zilla most of the time. I was always sure that if Harold Robson had been free to marry her, she wouldn't have given him a second glance," went on Mrs. Ash.

Margaret was silent for a little while, then she said very gravely:

"I wonder what really made her join the Army. Something has happened to her, Mother. I wish you would go down and have a talk with her. I can't get so far myself now, or I would go."

"Well of course, the news in the papers about Green and that poor man who plays the organ here, I always forget his name," said her mother.

"Acland."

Mrs. Ash rolled her fountain pen to and fro on the table.

"Is the door shut? Come and sit here beside me on the couch. I think I can do no good, but might do harm, by going down," said Mrs. Ash finally, in a very low tone, "there are some things best left alone, Margaret."

"Mother!" protested Margaret.

But Mrs. Ash only motioned her to speak more quietly. "That leather coat, for instance," she whispered.

"Mother," came again in sharp indignant protest.

Mrs. Ash only nodded her head slowly and gravely.

"But this is dreadful! Impossible!" said Margaret. "You talk as if . . . as though . . . Zilla's not mixed up with the tragedy," she added also in a whisper. "Except as we all are, we who knew Annabelle."

"If you want to help Zilla," her mother repeated, "don't press me for explanations, or for confidences. Leave her aside—out of all this—I'm thankful that she has done just what she has done. Zilla has had the wit, and the pluck, to get herself where she now is. For God's sake leave her strictly alone. She knows what she's doing, and why. We don't, can't, and, perhaps, musn't. Now, let's never speak of this again. But I had to warn you, for Zilla's sake, to let well enough alone." Her mother picked up her pen.

"But surely Harold doesn't feel like this—I mean about her." Margaret felt as though she must be in a nightmare.

"No, no! And, of course, with him, I kept to the outside of things. That I didn't think Zilla could make him the right wife . . . That she had been swept off her feet in the past . . . because of difficulty of getting him!" finished Mrs. Ash in quite her old tone.

Margaret was glad to leave her mother to herself.

Meantime the chief constable had been locking away Clarkson's report and the copies of the evidence given by Whitehouse. He stood reread the latter. Something in his silence made his nephew ask, "What's unsatisfactory about it?"

"I don't know," was the reply: "But Whitehouse's story as to how he got away is a very thin affair," said Findlay slowly. "And he omitted mention of where he spent last night. Oh, I agree," he replied to Tyrwhitt's expression. "Quite so, that might easily be explained. But, taken in conjunction with the fact that his story, from the moment he left Hawkstone, doesn't fit in with a thing we can find out—it's not so good."

"But surely, as that's all after, not before, doesn't matter much—" His uncle did not reply for a moment, then he asked:

"Has it ever struck you, Geoff, that, both times when a murder was done, Whitehouse was away according to his own story, but not as proven by any alibi?"

"Yet you don't suspect Robson, and the same is true of him," Tyrwhitt pointed out.

"Oh no, it isn't the same. Robson has an alibi, this last time, according to your time-table. And the first time, Uthwatt's evidence was very nearly an alibi. Then too, he lost far too heavily by his wife's death just then, not to have put it off a day or so. He knew his father-in-law was on his deathbed.

"But Whitehouse," went on Findlay, "profited enormously by the first murder, and he profits again if this second murder can be pinned to Green. I wish that chief inspector could look into it. But of course, it's Exeter's, not our say-so now.

"In this case, just supposing there's anything in the idea, then the woodman was recognized by Whitehouse, if not by Green, and Whitehouse at once saw the importance of there being a link, however slight, between Acland and Green, if Green was to be made to look like Acland's murderer."

"Supposing him to have been on the spot, Whitehouse could have murdered Acland, and got away, before I rushed down the stairs and out to the garden house," agreed Tyrwhitt, "though he would have had to work fast; but Green would have been on the spot in one bound; the French doors were open into the living room where he was. Granted, he had his back to the window for a moment having a drink. Even a long moment, yet the hat was slashed and put on the dead man after he was killed. That couldn't have been done before Green was out there.

You forget that scream Acland gave—poor devil. There simply wasn't time."

"I know," said Findlay, lighting a cigar very carefully.

"I see your meaning," Tyrwhitt caught it, "you mean, Acland may have been killed first, and the hat put on him to make those in the house think it was Whitehouse, and then Whitehouse gave that ghastly screech when it suited him? But Whitehouse would have been detected. No one could have got away."

"There is one more point," said Findlay "The surgeon who made the autopsy doesn't think that any man could have cried out after that blow hit him."

"He screamed when he saw it coming," suggested Tyrwhitt.

"The blow was too straight fore and aft for that to be likely. Besides, the position of his feet show that he had not risen or turned."

Tyrwhitt said that no surgeon could be sure that Acland had not caught a glimpse of the descending hand or weapon.

"Well, there it is," murmured the chief constable. He locked the papers away.

"What about Robson taking Whitehouse along with him?" asked Tyrwhitt.

"Rather like asking a cobra to stay with you, you think? But Robson will be quite safe as long as Whitehouse thinks we believe that we have the murderer of Mrs. Robson and of Acland safely under lock and key. Which was why I very carefully did not examine him on his statement."

"I see. Yes, I suppose it'll be all right."

"Just so, and as both are staying together, we can watch them easier, one to be protected, and one to be investigated. Should I be right, and if he thought we suspected him, Whitehouse would be a very dangerous man."

Pointer attended the inquest at Exeter on Acland.

The verdict was a foregone conclusion, and, at its end Green, who maintained his innocence, was found guilty, and was formally arrested.

Most of the people interested in the first murder, the indirect cause of this second one, were present at the inquest. Zilla Ash had been allowed special leave for the occasion, and listened intently to the proceedings.

When they were over, the verdict of murder recorded, and Green duly arrested, Tyrwhitt, who had come down to be able to give his uncle a firsthand account of the proceedings, walked back to his hotel with Pointer. They talked a while of the inquest they had just left, at least Tyrwhitt talked, Pointer was very silent.

"My uncle has learned that Acland was an out-and-out blackmailer. Learned it unofficially, but quite certainly, from people who won't come forward, but whom he has been bleeding systematically. In a way, it makes his murder fit in with anyone having done it. By the way, another little knot to undo, Zilla Ash was away from home when Acland was murdered, and the relatives whom her people think she was stopping with in London weren't in town at the time. And I can add another little gem to your collection. I seem to have the knack of seeing Zilla when she's off duty. I saw her, and Whitehouse, having a couple of drinks not half an hour ago, their heads together, and talking in whispers. Yet she acted, when I saw them together at the police station the day of The Clearing murder, as though she had hardly spoken to him, as though he were merely an acquaintance of her parents. And, as far as we know, they have not met since they both came in there to make their statements and sign them."

"How did they part? It's the parting that often tells everything to the onlooker."

"They parted like lovers, holding hands, as though each hated to see the other go. I must say she looked splendid. For the first time I agree with my uncle that she has a beautiful face, as well as a beautiful figure."

"I believe you're in love with her yourself!" Pointer laughed.

Tyrwhitt thrust out his right hand with the two fingers extended, Neapolitan-wise. "May the saints protect us from witchcraft! No. But now, is this extraneous, or integral?"

Pointer gave a smile. "It's interesting either way," he conceded as he left him.

He wanted a word with Whitehouse. He found him, naturally enough, full of the inquest. But he was still as vague as ever about his own whereabouts after he left Hawkstone. Pointer had no official standing in the case, and did not try to get him to be more precise. He brought the talk around to Annabelle Robson as soon as possible.

"About your first meeting with Mrs. Robson in England, you say in your statement that you made sure of her identity," Pointer said next.

"Oh, by every test," broke in Whitehouse with a laugh, "no chance on earth of her not being Annabelle Bigger, Chief Inspector."

"Just so. You say in evidence that she was confined to her room the day you got there. Now, thinking back carefully, when did you go to Thoresway?"

"Sometime in early September, I think—yes, early September."

The Lincoln police had got the date from the Inn. It had been on September the fifth.

"You had written first to the Robsons?"

"Oh no! The idea was that I was to drop in without giving any warning, and see for myself how things were."

"Her parents thought she was not happy?"

"She was always a poor correspondent, but her letters were getting shorter, and shorter, and more and more widely spaced. My aunt, one of the kindest and best of souls, could not understand it. Annabelle told me she was dog tired and too heart-sick to write home. Not heartsick from anything to do with Harold, but from the dreadful unceasing toil, with no prospect of anything different for ever and ever—I'm quoting her own words."

"I see. Now, going back to your arrival in Thoresway, you took a room at the inn?"

"No. I got there in time for lunch, and then asked the way to a place called The Clearing. Found Harold just coming out of the gate with some sugar beet he wanted the local Council to test. There was no mistake about his being glad to see me. The day before he had found Annabelle in a dead faint on the floor and put her to bed. She told him she had caught her arm in the hinge of the gate, and though it didn't show much, was having a lot of pain with it. But he thought it was also overwork, and being dead tired. At the moment, the aspirin he had given her was taking effect and she had fallen asleep. Things were going badly with them. They had made up their minds to sell out, and he was negotiating for a purchaser at the moment. We went back to the car, and had a long talk. After which he decided to run up to town and stop the sale—which was for a ruinous price—proceeding further. When Annabelle was well enough to see me, she was as delighted as Harold to have a talk over old days. Poor Annabelle, you could tell how homesick she had been!"

"Just a moment," said Pointer, "exactly how many days was it after your arrival, before you saw Mrs. Robson at The Clearing? Please think carefully. It may be most important."

Whitehouse sat a moment in deep reflection. "Let me see," he began to murmur days and think them over . . . "Tuesday I got there . . . she was in bed. I was in town over the weekend with friends . . . till the next Tuesday . . . It was the next day but one. Thursday. That's right." He went over his calculations again. "It was Tuesday when I got there, and Thursday week when I saw Mrs. Robson. I had no idea it was so long. Green could have told you in a minute," he added. "He's a wonderful memory. But I know I'm right."

Pointer sat a moment staring at his shoes. So he was right. There was a gap in the orderly hum drum life of Annabelle Robson as she was known at The Clearing . . . there had been over ten days . . . perhaps a good deal over . . . three weeks possibly . . . when another side of Annabelle Robson had started something that had led to her horrible end at The Clearing.

Looking up, he asked about Morris, and told the apparently very shocked and surprised Whitehouse about the man's suicide. Whitehouse repeated what Pointer already knew of the chance meeting in the Savoy.

Whitehouse had known the Millers slightly, and gave the same account as had Robson of their fate. Their only child was a girl called Ada. As to 'Posey' being her nickname, he repeated that his acquaintance with the whole family was not a close one.

"I was told that Mrs. Robson disliked Acland," Pointer said "What caused this, do you know?"

"She said it had no reason, at first she just couldn't bear the fellow. But later, it was because he was always trying to talk to her when she would meet him out, and invariably wanted to see her home, always cadging invitations to the house. She complained to Harold, finally, and he was very angry—as any husband would be, at the fellow's damn cheek."

"And you disliked him too?"

"On sight—just without any reason, and, like her, I soon had sufficient reason—when twice I found him in the house on my unexpected return."

"When was this?"

Whitehouse could only give the times vaguely. It was between the two last quarter visits of the Robsons, was all that he could say for certain. He had been afraid at the time that the man might be after some of the papers sent him, which occasionally were highly confidential, and contained useful statistics.

"Though now I realize that he may have had an appointment with Green. It's my private belief—and

probably yours too—that Acland was blackmailing Green
for something in his past. I never bothered to look up
Green's references. He was damned good as a private
secretary, and I had nothing of any value in the early
days—the confidential papers came much later. I gave
him a trial, and very soon would have been lost without
him. I should have thought him the last type ever to be
violent. Had a temper, nothing could ruffle, I thought."

"You think Acland came on those two occasions to see
Green?"

"Probably. But, as it happened, by chance, both
occasions Green was out."

"Did Acland ever go upstairs?"

"Not to my knowledge. But as the back door was never
locked, it's quite possible he may have been over the
house many times."

"You never found Acland and Green talking together?"

"Not except of an evening at the pub."

"Now about this man, Morris, in whom I'm interested.
I hold that he must have been in love with Mrs. Robson,
whether with, or without her knowledge. For only a love
affair can explain his killing himself. Everything else in
his life seems absolutely at variance with the idea. Only
some heart-breaking news can account for it—we think.
And his death was on the night following Mrs. Robson's
murder. If it wasn't about an unfortunate love affair, then
there's absolutely no reason for him to have done it, and
one would have to suspect foul play. On the other hand,
Green's defence will certainly produce that paper Morris
left on the table in his room, and will try to maintain that
Morris killed Mrs. Robson, and then himself. If they can
find anything on which to rest that idea we must be
prepared to meet it, too."

"If Green is going to try and cheat Justice by setting
up either Acland or Morris as the murderer, Chief
Inspector, I'll certainly help you to the best of my ability.
And I'll tell you this. There was something odd about that
meeting at the Savoy—the only time I ever saw the two

together —something that didn't ring true. It's hard to put a vague feeling into words, and, possibly, if she hadn't been killed, and he hadn't killed himself, I might not have given it another thought, but as things are . . . I don't believe they had met as they said they had. And Annabelle kept breaking in—prompting him—one might almost have called it. Annabelle was a frank creature, still, in some ways, not a woman of the world skilled in duplicity, and she didn't do it too convincingly—so it now seems to me."

There was a short pause, then he went on.

"But I don't for a moment think there was any love affair between the two. I think they really had met that night quite by chance, after a long interval of not seeing each other. I thought there was a willingness to revive an old flirtation on her side, but not on his. He looked ill at ease, and I don't think he cared for the fling."

"His manner may have been due to resentment at the length of the interval during which he and Mrs. Robson had seen nothing of each other," suggested Pointer.

Whitehouse said that he could only say that that was not the impression which he had received.

"Was Mrs. Robson truthful?" Pointer asked bluntly.

Whitehouse looked awkward. "I think some women, nice women mind you, have a different idea of what truth is, from men," he said evasively.

"Let's put it like this. If Mrs. Robson and her husband both told you something quite contradictory, whom would you believe?"

"Oh, Harold, of course, I see what you mean. Well, then, between ourselves, my cousin—well, I can't call her anything but a dreadful little liar of late. She became a frightful snob, and insisted more and more on telling one personal details of Lady This and the Duchess of That of which she could only have learned in some silly papers, but which she retailed as her personal knowledge. She was growing a vain, selfish, and bad-tempered woman—all through that fortune."

"Aren't you afraid of your own character deteriorating, now it has come to you?" Pointer asked blandly.

"I am going to marry a strong-minded girl who will keep me straight," laughed Whitehouse.

"Any particular lady in mind?" asked Pointer lightly.

Whitehouse hesitated for a moment. "I see no reason why you shouldn't know, but keep it under your hat for a while. I asked Miss Ash this morning to marry me and she consented. We're sending the notice in shortly, and will be married during her next leave, and I shall then get a job nearer her."

Pointer congratulated him briefly.

A War Office car had drawn up. The chief inspector had been offered a lift back to town by an officer who had been inspecting the Exeter Home Guard. Zilla Ash would follow next in an A.T.S. truck which Pointer had asked the police to detain for about half an hour after his own start, if possible. That, delay, and the speed of the car he was in, would give him ample time to get to her barracks in Town.

He had promised the Exeter police to look up anything that he thought might have a bearing on the events at Hawkstone, and he believed that Zilla might well have been down there, when she was supposed to be staying with friends in Town, just before she joined the A.T.S.

He had a word over the telephone with those in authority. As the result he was grudgingly allowed to inspect the suitcase of civilian clothes which Zilla Ash had stored in the luggage room. Pointer thought it just possible that, knowing its usual inviolability, Zilla might have left in it things she would not care to store at home. As there was the possibility that she had been the one to batter Annabelle Robson's face, it had to be looked into.

He could not understand why the Lincoln police had not searched her rooms., and that of her sister, at once. There were only a few things in the suitcase which Zilla had been carrying when she had walked into the barracks and asked to be allowed to change from her egg-round to Army Service.

Nothing in the clothing interested Pointer, but this was not true of a crumpled scrap of paper in the pocket of her tweed coat. It was a pencilled scribble on the edge, torn from a newspaper, giving the trains from Taunton to Paddington, and there was no mistaking, to his trained eye, Acland's curious, spidery writing. He put it carefully away in an envelope.

The only other item that interested him was a brass from a cart horse's collar. An Exeter brass, modern and poor in workmanship. Acland's cart had been found at the door of his aunt's, stable the morning after Acland's murder, in Tiverton. The horse had come home during the night. One of the brasses from his collar was missing. The brass at which Pointer was now looking, he felt sure. Pointer gave a receipt for the brass and sat down to wait. So Zilla Ash was linked with Acland who had been murdered, as well as with Annabelle Robson who had been murdered.

In half an hour Zilla came into the room. They were alone.

"I have just had a look through your belongings, Miss Ash," he began. "And I want you to explain this paper"— he held it out on the palm of one hand, but kept the fingers of the other hand on its edges.

"I'm much too well brought up to snatch," said Zilla affably, giving it one casual glance. "I picked that up in the road, along with a horse-brass. You have it too, of course?"

"I have. The writing on that paper is Mr. Acland's. The brass is one missing from his horse."

"Indeed!" drawled Zilla, and said no more, but sat down on a bench near the window.

"And where did you pick them up'?" asked Pointer coldly.

"On the road, the road between Tiverton and Taunton."

"And was it you who lured Mr. Acland to that chair in the summerhouse?" he asked.

Zilla turned quite white, even to her firm, very red lips. "I see," she said under her breath. "That's the idea, is it?"

"Can you give us a better one?" he countered. She sat, stroking the back of one slender hand with the other.

"I chanced on that paper in the road, as I was bicycling from Taunton to Tiverton, and as I saw that it gave the trains I was myself going to ask about, I kept it. I picked up the brass because I have a few in my sitting room at home and wanted to add the new one, poor though it is, because I had found it myself—like finding a horseshoe, you know—" her color had returned. She seemed quite herself again.

"And the date when this happened?"

"Let me see. It was Saturday the 7th when Annabelle Robson was killed—"

"Murdered," he corrected sternly.

"It was Wednesday when Harold Robson spoke about having come on something which made him guess where Green must be with Mr. Whitehouse, and the day after that, Thursday I found a parcel in Whitehouse's writing' addressed to my sister, sent from Biddiscombe. So I knew that I had a good chance of meeting both men if I hurried. I went up to town and spent the night there. I with friends then took an early train for Tiverton the next morning.

"When I got to Tiverton in the afternoon I taxied out to Hawkstone. Thought it all looked very peaceful, and decided Harold had been getting the wind up quite needlessly, so I decided not to push myself in. A girl has her pride, you know—Chief Inspector." Zilla's face was positively prim as she spoke. "But, as the weather was wonderful, and I hadn't had a holiday for donkey's years, I decided to stay around, say nothing, and see if anything happened. I expected to meet Harold or Reg, of course."

"Reg?" Pointer seemed puzzled.

"Mr. Whitehouse's first name is Reginald," she explained. "But I never ran into either, and so I got bored stiff, and decided to return to town, and home and eggs. But those thrilling posters on the way down spoiled that. You know the poster where the soldier, the sailor, and the airman are getting into a train in full kit, and all looking at the girl standing on the platform? It's really devastating. I decided to join up, and get a wave form the lads, not a mere stare. I think it was Saturday morning— yes it was, that I picked up the paper, and the brass, and did a bit of walking for my figure's sake till I met a car which drove me half way to town. I bought a suitcase and arrived at the barracks here. That's everything I can tell you."

"You'll be on an oath in the witness box," said Pointer carelessly. "And what you say will be investigated."

"I can take it," she replied stolidly. "Anything else?"

"Yes, what did Mrs. Robson tell you about a man called Morris, George Morris?"

Zilla lent forward with exaggerated interest "A man? Annabelle? I wish I could help you out with scandal, officer. But she never revealed any of her heart's secrets to me."

"You are talking of a murdered woman," Pointer said rigidly, his eyes very hard

"That doesn't alter her character, utterly mean, and superficial, and"—she pulled herself with a visible effort. "I didn't care for Annabelle Robson, Chief Inspector, and the fact that someone else couldn't stand her either, doesn't alter her character."

"But you never heard the name Morris mentioned by anyone, at The Clearing, or connected with people there?"

"Never as a person, only as a car," she said.

CHAPTER ELEVEN

When Pointer had gone, Zilla went to the telephone and rang up her mother. She had told Whitehouse that she must be the one to let the Ashes know the news of their engagement. Mrs. Ash received the announcement in dead silence.

"Mother! Didn't you hear? I thought you'd be so pleased! By the way, my C.O. here is, Kitty Bramwell, that toad's sister. She adores men with large fortunes, and she's wild with rage. I told her first of all, and asked her whether I might wear my engagement ring in uniform. I shall have to wear a glove over it at night, or the wardens will be after me to 'put out that light'. It really is stunning. It stunned Kitty, all right! Now look, I'm on convoy duty, leaving this morning for the north, and I've wangled two days' leave, beginning tomorrow, which I want to spend with you at home. Of course, Reginald wants to ask your blessing in person, so I've invited him to lunch the second day. That be all right?"

"It's not possible to discuss this over the telephone," said her mother coldly, "there are many points to be considered."

"Too late, darling. It's all arranged, including his coming to lunch."

"Mr. Robson is in Thoresway at the moment," her mother went on by way of a reply.

"Ask him to lunch tomorrow. Reg won't be there till the next day. I shall be with you by about ten in the morning, and I must have a talk with him."

"As to having Harold Robson to lunch when you're here—"

But Zilla overrode her mother's objections. Privately, Mrs. Ash thought that even Zilla might well want a final talk in person with the man she used to chase so persistently when he represented something out of her reach.

Robson accepted for lunch. He had just come in when Zilla entered, gave him a cool, lifeless hand and started talking about her new life. Even she, however, kept the talk away from the recent happenings at Exeter, and did not once mention Whitehouse. Her parents were careful to give no hint of the new engagement.

As soon as the meal was over, Zilla turned to Robson. "I want a word with you, Harold. Suppose we have our coffee in the morning room." She handed him her cup as well as his own, and led the way with her shoulders very square. He said goodbye to his hostess and host, adding that he must leave in a very few minutes. A short time after they heard the front door shut, and his steps going down the gravel drive.

Zilla sauntered in, cigarette in hand.

"Well, are you pleased about me and Reg?" she asked.

"Was Robson pleased?" her father countered.

"Delighted," drawled Zilla. "He as good as told me that he had only given in to me so as to save me from dying of a broken heart. And now he knows that he is free of me for good. But aren't you pleased, mother? As I said on the phone I thought, you'd love it."

Her father stamped out of the room muttering. Mrs. Ash waited till he had shut the door.

"Green will be tried this early autumn," she said. "It will be a painful case. You will be cited, of course, as a witness—"

"I shall be overseas," said Zilla promptly.

"I doubt if you will be allowed to leave this country."

"Well, what will be—will be." Zilla lit a cigarette.

"Yes," Mrs. Ash spoke gravely, "but what about this idea of marrying Mr. Whitehouse?"

"As soon as my next leave comes around."

Zilla suddenly came to her mother's side. "I'm fond of him," she said simply, "and—well—I shall make him a good wife. I shall really, mother. I find I want quiet—and peace—after all."

"But oughtn't you to wait till this trial is over? Is it fair to him," said Mrs. Ash. "All sorts of things are dragged in—and dragged out—at such a trial." Mrs. Ash was not looking at Zilla, and Zilla stared down at the carpet.

"I can take it," she said after a moment's pause. "Believe me, mother, nothing can come out that you and Reg don't know already—and that holds for Kitty Bramwell," she added.

"You're often over-confident of your own powers," said her mother.

"The Army is sweating that out of me," laughed' Zilla, and tried to switch the talk to a debate on where she and Reginald would live after the war.

But Mrs. Ash refused to follow the red herring. "I've got to say something very unpleasant," she said instead. "I think you're quite mad to stir up all the mud that will be stirred up if you marry Mr. Whitehouse. It may come out about your one time infatuation for Mr. Robson. Add to that, however, that you switch over your affections to the man to whom the money comes—and what do you expect people to say?"

"What they damn well like!"

"Mad!" muttered Mrs. Ash. "Then there's another point—Mr. Whitehouse is by no means completely cleared of all suspicion by Mr, Green's arrest—by no means completely. People hint at its being very convenient for him that his cousin didn't live another twenty four hours even. You're drawn into the death of Annabelle Robson by that coat she passed on to you—the burnt coat—and if you marry the man who profits so enormously by that death—again think of the kind of talk there will be."

"I don't care that for gossip!" Zilla snapped her slender, but very strong fingers like a whip.

"Everybody will cut you," her mother continued.

Zilla made a grimace.

"Then one last thing. Suppose Mr. Whitehouse did know something about Annabelle's murder? Do you care for the position of a murderer's wife?"

It was characteristic of Zilla Ash that she listened to this talk with complete good nature. It did not make enough impression to ruffle her temper.

When Whitehouse arrived the next morning, he and Mr. Ash had a long, private talk. Then Whitehouse went in search of Zilla, and Ash looked in on his wife.

"Well, my dear, Whitehouse is making an absolutely princely settlement on Zilla. I must say she's doing well for herself. There's only one thing I don't quite care about. He wants to give Robson one third of the Australian money, I think that's a bit quixotic."

The telephone rang. Major Findlay wanted to know whether Mr. Whitehouse was still at Ing's Place? Then would Mr. Ash be so kind as to ask him when he could look in at the police station and have a word with Chief Inspector Pointer who would be waiting there? As a matter of fact, a car would be passing in a few minutes, the driver had been told to see if he could take Whitehouse on from Ing's Place. Whitehouse left in it. He looked a little uncomfortable as he shook, hands with the impassive man from Scotland Yard.

"Exeter wants a fuller story of your getting away from Hawkstone, Mr. Whitehouse, and of the part in it played by your fiancée. We know she helped you." Pointer meant that he guessed as much.

"I'm glad," said Whitehouse, apparently sincerely, "I can't think why she insists on keeping it all so dark. She saved my life."

"Now will you tell me, in your own words, just what happened while you were down at Hawkstone ?"

"No objections whatever," said Whitehouse, "it was only my promise to Zilla that had kept me silent. Well, I suppose she has told you how she herself felt certain that I might be in danger, when she heard that Green and I had got away, and decided to follow? She suddenly stepped into the sitting room at Hawkstone that afternoon, and begged me to get away at once. Green was out shopping for food, and she didn't know Robson had already come down. She was very urgent, in dead earnest, and told me that she had a plan for getting me to London. She would come to fetch me the following day. You see, neither she nor I had the slightest notion that Robson was in the house with us, or we needn't have acted as we did. When she had slipped away again, I felt lonely, I noticed too how little freedom I had. I couldn't have gone to the village without Green coming with me, he always gave my safety as the reason, but Miss Ash had made me begin to notice things. . . . He was making no effort to get servants for the house. I found that he had not telephoned to a registry office in Exeter when he said he had. . . . Next morning I was ready for her when she came to the summerhouse. She had arranged with the woodman to hire his cart. She, not he, had driven up in it, and left it round the first bend on the road, out of sight. I had packed a bag with a few necessities in it, had a word with the woodman, whose identity I never suspected, and slipped out, after her. She threw a cloth around my shoulders, and drew one of these waterproof caps over my head and face, which, with the cloth around my shoulders, made me look like a very stout woman huddled beside her in the cart. Horses are one of the things I can manage, and we got near to Taunton, when we saw police patrols in the road. Zilla never turned a hair, took the reins, and drove on, her head bare. They weren't on the lookout for two women, and barely glanced at us. At Taunton she got out, left the horse in a side lane, made me tidy up, and stopped a car, asking for a lift to our child, ill in hospital at Chard. At Chard she used to stay with friends at the manor. She knew the local garage well, got a car, and was able to get a local farmer friend to help out." At Chard, she had bought some plain velvet Curtain stuff, and it was with this velvet wrapped around

him, and a hood down over his head, that Whitehouse
had gone into London. The two had then parted.

"When did you first know of Acland's murder?" asked
Pointer.

"Passing through Clapham, the evening papers were
out, and she bought one. That was where we separated in
a tea shop, which I entered, in my usual garb of course."

"What did she say about Acland's murder?"

"It stunned her. Absolutely stunned her. She and I
both thought—and think—that Green was only after me.
We had no idea he could make the mistake that he did. It
was Acland's putting on my white panama hat that was
the real cause of his death, for I think all that about the
cut being too small is nonsense."

Pointer thanked him, and watched him sign his
statement. He could now have that talk with Robson on
which in his opinion so much depended. Whitehouse's
statement of the time that had elapsed after his arrival at
the inn, before he had actually met his cousin, had given
Pointer the lever which he was now, going to use to pry
the lid of Robson's determined silence. He was driven
onto Grantham, where he had arranged with Robson to
have a talk with him.

Robson evidently thought it would be about the events
at Exeter, and for a time they discussed Acland's murder,
then Pointer said that it really had nothing to do with his
search into the causes of Morris' death.

"Are you still working on that? But I thought the
inquest—" said Robson, opening his eyes.

"—Means nothing, except that a body can be buried,"
said Pointer to that. "I still link his death with that of
your wife in the morning, and so I want to know where
Mrs. Robson was during the time that she was away from
The Clearing."

Robson half rose from his chair, but Pointer, waved
him down.

"It's no use taking it that way, Mr. Robson, that won't
help us. Unless it was murder—it was an old love for her.

We now believe, and have good reasons for the belief, that Mrs. Robson was away from home when Mr. Whitehouse arrived. That is the only time, as I see it, when Morris could have met her and fallen in love with her."

"You! You!" Robson was unable to get words out. Pointer held up his hand to quiet the man.

"Not she with him, Mr. Robson. There's never a hint in all this, at any time, of her caring in the least for anyone but yourself. But we think she met him while she was away from The Clearing during that couple of weeks. Without it we can't feel sure it was suicide, and so I think I can promise that we shall find it all out. But you could help us to save time. We know she was away from Clearing, you see."

Robson took a turn up and down the long room, still without speaking. At last he sat down and faced the other.

"Yes, she did leave The Clearing," he said at last, speaking under his breath, "it broke even her down. That's why I was trying to sell it when Reg turned up."

"Did you know she was going?" asked Pointer.

"No. I found her in the house in a dead faint one day, and put her to bed. She hurt her arm in the gate, and I was a bit short about it. Couldn't see any cut or bruise and said as much. Next day, I didn't see her out working, when I got back from the market where I had been selling some roots, and didn't find her in the house. But I found a letter on the table saying that she was going to London, she had a little money of her own left, to have a rest, the first in all these years. She would let me know where she was staying as soon as she found rooms, she wrote. That was all. Next day came Reg. I couldn't let him in on it. Couldn't. Not at once. And the next day came another letter from my wife that altered everything. Even the one day's rest had made a difference. I went to the address she gave me, and we decided that we would sell The Clearing—if we could. Meantime, she was to have as long a rest as she needed, and then come home for the last lap—which wouldn't be long, we both hoped. Next day I went back. Annabelle was most insistent that Reg shouldn't know she had had to give up. She always was like that even as a child. When she was well enough, I got a car, and drove her back from town. We very happy to be together again. I promised faithfully that I wouldn't ever refer to her leaving me. Never, no more partings for us, and Reg's news had given us fresh hope. I still wanted to sell, but she didn't, and it was her money, you see, from start to finish. So we didn't sell, but arranged matters so that she got help in the fields and the house. It was a second honeymoon," he said slowly. "Now, Chief Inspector, you tell me that Morris and she met during that time? I neither know nor care. Annabelle hadn't eyes for anyone but me, that I do know."

Pointer again said that everyone knew as much, and asked for Annabelle's address in town, as this ought to be a help in linking up with Morris.

Robson gave it, but added that it had been blitzed, and his wife had then moved to a house that was still standing, when last he heard about it. He let Pointer have both addresses.

Pointer had got what he needed. He looked long at his shoe tips as the train carried him to London. There he verified that the first address, a lodging house in a very cheap part of town, had had a direct hit, fortunately with no loss of life, as most of the people had taken refuge in the shelter, but the present whereabouts of the late landlady was unknown. The second address was in a much better locality. Evidently the arrival of help from Australia had made its effect felt already though only as a promise. The landlady remembered the Robsons perfectly. Yes, Mrs. Robson had stayed there for only a little over a week, but since then, whenever the Robsons came to town, they put up at her rooms, "though I don't suppose they'll come here much longer. They were getting too grand for us. At least she was. But there—it was only natural, wasn't it?"

"It's about Mr. Morris that I've really come," Pointer explained chattily that he was in a solicitor's office, and, that his firm wanted to get into touch with a George Morris who had been a friend of Mrs. Robson's. The landlady said she didn't know the name, but then, she didn't know the name of any of Mrs. Robson's friends.

"But we're sure he met her when she was first here—you know, just after the house where she was staying had been blitzed."

The landlady knew all about the blitzed lodgings, but still denied all knowledge of Morris, or any other visitor to Mrs. Robson than her husband.

"One of these is Mr. Morris' picture, but it's—it's—well, it was taken after he died and we're not sure which is his."

He showed her six, all truly dreadful ones, of dead men.

The landlady studied all without any show of emotion She picked out the one of George Morris. "I seem to remember his face—I don't know any of the others—but I can't place it—Oh, I know it's *him*! Yes, I feel sure it's *him*! Yes I'll swear it's *him*!"

"Good!" said Pointer, "'but, why do you call him 'him' like that?"

"It's what she called him the once when he passed. Mrs. Robson was just going out, talking back to me as she was leaving, when to my surprise she bounces back into the hall, and slams the front door shut in a great hurry. 'It's *him*!' she says as though frightened 'My goodness, what shall I do?' and she runs into this room we're in, and peers through the curtains. Of course I had a look too. A gentleman, that one there," the landlady indicated the photograph, "was passing on the other side and staring at all the houses as he passed. 'Oh dear!' says Mrs. Robson shrinking back. 'He mustn't find me! Oh, what shall I do if he comes here?' But he walked on, and after a bit, Mrs. Robson quiets down. She said it was someone she used to know in Australia, to whom she was all but engaged when Mr. Robson turned up, and they fell in love with each other at first sight and were married in a great hurry. She never told me this other one's name, so I remember him just as 'him'. She never referred to him again, nor did I."

He learned nothing more from her. So Morris had had a definite place in Annabelle Robson's past life. She had acted, at least the once, as though afraid of him—but, as she had seemed pleased to see him at the Savoy, and had looked him up at his office—without, Pointer thought, letting her husband know—her fear was more likely to be an anxiety to avoid his meeting her just then. A strange little puzzle. Pointer thought of what the chief constable had said about this being a case where everything had two answers. Annabelle Robson, who had seemed to dread meeting Morris the one time, had seemed to welcome it when they met.

Pointer had already looked up the address given by Bernard Morris as that of his brother's first shop at the time of Mrs. Robson's visit to London. He had tried at each of them for any link with the dead woman—with any woman. But the dead man seemed to have kept his social affairs quite separate from his businesses. He seemed liked at every place, and, as far as lay in his power, had kept his old employees. But there was no trace of Annabelle Robson or of Posey. His next efforts were to make quite sure of Whitehouse's *bona fides*. There was a possibility, however farfetched it seemed, that a gang was at work here, that Annabelle, her husband, and Whitehouse, were all in a plot together, each vouching for the other's identity in order to secure the big fortune in Australia. But he found that Whitehouse was quite well known at his bank and at Australia House, and was quite definitely the Whitehouse that he claimed to be, and the same was true of Annabelle and Harold Robson, though in a much smaller way. The bank manager had met him and his father in

Canberra, and Annabelle had had to come in several times of late about the fortune left her.

There was to be no easy way out of the tangle, Pointer saw. And yet there must be some connection—so his reason told him—between the secret, hidden, Annabelle Robson and her battered face. Pointer then, for the present, accepted the mutilation as part of the murderer's plan, and so it could have but the one meaning—prevention of identification. Not of Annabelle Robson as Robson's wife but as—as whom? He looked carefully through Whitehouse's statement. Had known Annabelle in Canberra since she was a baby. . . last seen her when she was seventeen years old. . . met again in Thoresway when she was twenty three. . . It was not possible that he could have been mistaken in Annabelle. And it was against his own interests to pass off a false, a counterfeit Annabelle as the real one. Annabelle stood in the way of his inheriting the Australian fortune. Here for once was a lock that Pointer could not seem to open, whatever key he tried. He had another couple of visits to make connected with the recent events. The Thoresway vicar had come down to the inquest on Acland, his organist, and was now on his way back, together with Uthwatt, who was one of his church wardens. Mr. Yeats had Pointer shown into his bedroom at the London hotel.

"About the Robsons—dear me, that's very ancient history for you at the Yard surely, Chief Inspector?" he began. Pointer said his piece about another name having cropped up, the name of a George Morris, a friend of Mrs. Robson. Had the rector ever heard of it either from her, or from anyone else, in The Clearing circle? Mr. Yeats had not. The talk then ran again over the circle itself. Mr. Green, Yeats said, judging from the kind of stories he told, was a thoroughly immoral man in every sense of the word. Robson, Yeats respected as a sharp business man.

Whitehouse he liked. About Mrs. Robson, he was rather reticent. Pointer inferred, rightly, that he had not cared for her. Zilla Ash he considered a really abandoned young woman. Margaret and Mrs. Ash he praised highly. Pointer brought in the name of Acland—here Yeats said he had always been sorry for the man. "I can't believe he was ever a blackmailer. He was a strange, unhappy character, whom everyone seemed to dislike, quite without reason. I found him an excellent organist. Perhaps some of his gifts—for he had gifts, of a very unusual character—were too unusual to make him easy company. At times he could be a true clairvoyant, but it was a fitful endowment, quite out of his own power to control. Sometimes he could read your thought without wanting to, sometimes it went all wrong. But there is no doubt but that he felt something terrible was linked with The Clearing. Only, as often happens with seers, he got the time element wrong. He thought it was past, instead of near future. Between ourselves, that is why he went so often to the house—to get the impression clearer—"

"He seems to have kept very doubtful company before he came to you," said Pointer.

"That's quite possible. He was very keen to develop the psychic side of himself. I think evil is sometimes more forceful, more active, than goodness. I grant you that he took a—what shall I say—unbiased—attitude toward both evil and good. All he cared for was to get below the surface, by his strange, uncanny gifts, so as to exercise them. Not that they always functioned. The very hour when Mrs. Robson's terrible death was taking place, he was playing one of Bach's most cheerful cantatas. Little did I think, either, as I sat listening to him with real delight, what was happening so close by."

"Mr. Acland was playing at the very time?" Pointer repeated slowly.

"It was his practice morning. He started--always starts--at twelve, and went on till two. He needed no alibi, of course, but I told my old friend, Major Findlay, about the practice, just the same."

"Who got him the post with you?"

"Mr Uthwatt. He's one of our church wardens, you know. He had heard him while on holiday, and he recommended him most highly when he found he had come to Curtain Lindsey, as the local reporter editor." As to Mrs. Robson's absence from The Clearing, clearly Yeats was ignorant of it, his testimony was exactly that heard so often before. Devoted but overworked couple nearing exhaustion . . . timely appearance of help from home, unexpected and sudden change of fortune. And then, finding Mr. Uthwatt would not be in for half an hour or so, Pointer went for a walk meanwhile. This walk took him to the telephone, and a long distance word with Superintendent Clarkson.

Yes, said Clarkson, the rector was quite right. Acland had been practicing on the church organ before, during, and after the time of Mrs. Robson's murder.

So Acland could not have seen, or heard, anything of the actual murder. Yet he was believed to have been murdered by the guilty person to silence his blackmail. True, he might, as the Lincoln police believed, have already been blackmailing Green, though no proof of any previous connection between the two had been proven, but as to The Clearing murder, what could Acland have held over the murderer?

The crime was a single-handed one. Had Green or Whitehouse discussed it? And had Acland overheard them? But Whitehouse's banking account, which the police had asked him to allow them to inspect, showed no withdrawals, at any time, of any blackmailing size. The same was true of Green.

It looked to Pointer as though Acland had not been murdered for the motive which the Lincoln and the Exeter police held to be the true one. He returned, lost in thought, to the hotel, Uthwatt was waiting for him.

"Want to see me?" he asked.

Pointer explained that the London police were making inquiries about the death of a George Morris, who had been, apparently, a friend of the late Mrs. Robson. Had Uthwatt ever heard her speak of him?

The farmer said that he had not and added that he knew none of her lately made friends. The chief inspector then asked him to tell him again about his finding of Mrs. Robson's body, explaining that a hearing was very different from reading evidence.

It was the search of the house that interested Pointer the most. Annabelle might have heard some sound which made her send for Rover and so, it would probably have come from inside.

Uthwatt seemed to have no objection to giving details. He ran over the two searches quickly. The first with Robson, the second with the police. He referred to the sending down for the keys to the boxroom.

"What?" asked Pointer in surprise. "I thought you had searched it before?"

"It was locked then," said Uthwatt; "I called to Robson to burst it open the first time, and he said not to waste time on it. It was always locked. No one could be inside. And he was right. No one was." Uthwatt then continued as before. When he had finished, he gave Pointer a curious look. The man from Scotland Yard seemed quite lost in a brown study of his own shoes. That closed the interview, and, thanking him, the chief inspector went out of the hotel feeling as though he had suddenly been handed a magic torch.

CHAPTER TWELVE

Tyrwhitt met him on his way to the train for Lincoln.

"My uncle's delighted that you're going to put up with him. Are you prepared to give us your reading of the double murders?"

"We ought to clear up a lot by the day after tomorrow," Pointer said.

"Tomorrow we get to my uncle's—with luck. There's a big Home Guard scheme at the moment. Started yesterday, and finishes up day after tomorrow, at dawn. Thoresway, Curtain Lindsey, and all around, will be in great danger by tomorrow afternoon. I shall have to rush in and help with the defense, unless I've been shot as a spy before getting there. You will have to join in too."

Pointer excused himself. He intended to take a part, though perhaps a late one, but the less said about that the better.

He had asked Whitehouse to come to the Thoresway inn the next day, as he, Pointer, wanted to talk over all the information about the two murders. Robson intended anyway to go to Thoresway, to choose what of the furniture, if any, he wanted taken to his new home. Whitehouse hesitated, but finally agreed.

"You think talk will clear up many doubtful bits?" Tyrwhitt now asked curiously. "The burnt coat? The dog sent for? Your man's—Morris' suicide? Or isn't that included?"

"Properly understood, it's the clue to everything that happened," Pointer thought, but he only said that he expected the general talk would make everything quite clear.

Tyrwhitt was right about the Home Guard being out in full force. The roads from the station to the house of the chief constable rang with "Halt! Who goes there!"

Pointer was dropped at the police station, and there made sure, first of all, that Whitehouse, Robson and Uthwatt had all turned up in the neighborhood.

Pointer had a talk with the superintendent. He wanted two constables on duty at The Clearing all night, even though the Home Guard had taken it over, among many other places, "for the duration" of the scheme.

Pointer left immediately after dinner that night, and made his way on foot out of the chief constable's grounds. The chief constable had his own role in the scheme and Tyrwhitt decided to be a fifth columnist, acting at the last minute with designs against the Post Office. They all slunk out like so many criminals, and parted without a word at the gate. The Home Guard were thoroughly at work. Every house in the neighborhood was in turn besieged and defended. A sturdy figure of a man nipping through the gate at The Clearing was challenged from the bushes on either side.

"I'm Robson, the owner," he replied, startled

"Oh, no, you're not! You're a fifth columnist, sneaking in. Arrest him."

"Look here," said the man, in not too good a temper. "I *am* Robson. I have a right to enter my own house, surely!"

"Not without the password, you haven't," was the reply. "No password reached you? Then you're not the owner, but a spy. Shoot him, boys!"

An order which caused much mirth to the Home guards, but caused the arrested man to swear long and deep.

"Listen to that! He's a German," said one joker. "I distinctly rickernised two of the words."

"Well, he's for it in the morning," said another. "In the meantime to the guard room" And in spite of his by no means feigned resistance, the man was taken to the morning room and locked in. Suddenly the wailing, sobbing screech of an alert echoed over the village. Hardly had it sounded, then the enemy planes came swooping in. The reason for the murderous attack that followed was never known, whether they had been mistaken for one of the aerodromes which lay around the hamlet, or whether it was just chance. While it lasted, and it lasted two hours, Thoresway skies, and Thoresway houses and fields shook and trembled and crashed, and were a blaze of lights, and gun fire, and flares, and bombs coming down, and shells going up.

Pointer found Clarkson directing salvage operations near the inn where two dead bodies were being taken out.

"That's the two," said Clarkson. "No one else is missing."

"I want you to help me dig out another body," said Pointer "Yes, dead I'm sure. At The Clearing."

"The Clearing!" said the superintendent. "Well, we're finished here. But who's at The Clearing, bar the Home Guard? I'll come, of course, with you."

There was too much noise to talk, but they followed closely, each on the other. The way was long, but they made it, with many interruptions to put out incendiaries that fell all around them.

At the gate, they were challenged by one of Clarkson's men. The H.G. were gone to help on rescue work. Pointer led the way to the side of the garden where lay piled a heap of stones and bricks, glass and mortar that had been the greenhouse.

"Go very carefully, men. Very lightly with the spades It's a woman," Pointer said. He had a word with Clarkson as they worked, more than a word, whole sentence, several sentences, which made at officer grasp a spade too, and like Pointer, begin very carefully to shovel up the broken masses of debris.

"New kind of hand grenade did this," said one the diggers, "anyhow whatever it was, struck slanting, not straight down."

"We shall want a stretcher," said Clarkson. "Take a door off and bring it here." He and Pointer were now scooping the broken mortar away with their hands. The constable peered at what they were uncovering.

"It's a corpse!"—he fell back "That's not been killed tonight!"

"Silence," said Clarkson sharply. Then, he straightened.

"Who goes there," he shouted, but Pointer made a leap, a grab, and then came a struggle in the blackness. Then an enemy bomb dropped so close that all lay stunned for the moment by the detonation and the blast, but Pointer's hand was still locked on the arm of the man he had grasped, and, seconds later, Harold Robson, who had climbed out of the morning room window, was handcuffed by the grimy superintendent to himself, while the others continued, under Pointer's directions, to dig the remains of the woman who had been buried under the cement flooring.

"So you have proved that the woman who took the place of the original Annabelle Robson was a girl called Elizabeth Jenkins? Known as 'Posey' to her friends and the house agents where she worked?" said the assistant commissioner, as they were seated in his room.

"Yes, sir. And that is how Morris first met her. As Elizabeth Jenkins.

"We have photographs of Miss Jenkins, who is quite certainly the woman known as Annabelle Robson at The Clearing. Robson had of course, coached her about Annabelle and life in Australia—the pictures of Australia in her room had the names written on them—and he was always present when Whitehouse and she had those long talks about Australia, which Whitehouse thought proved the poor girl to have been so very homesick."

"I think the damaged right arm was invented to explain the difference in her handwriting till little by little people got used to the change," said Pointer.

"Evidently she didn't know the truth as to what had happened to the real wife," said the assistant commissioner.

"Quite evidently not, sir. Probably she was told some cock-and-bull story about Robson's wife having eloped with someone, and of Robson being about to lose a good thing through her being away just then. I suppose Elizabeth Jenkins was delighted, at first, with having a house of her own, she was an orphan we're told, and very hard up and apparently very much in love with Robson, who seems to have a strange fascination for women. He met her when he was putting The Clearing in the hands of several London agents for sale. Her coloring would have struck him by its amazing likeness to that of his wife which, of course, was what quite took in Whitehouse."

"She must have thought she was in for a very, good time when all that money came rolling along. I wonder she didn't stand in with Robson, even when she knew the truth."

"I think she might have, had he had time to put it to her. But he evidently burst in on her with that blood stained coat in her hand, when she was all riled up. He too was worked up at the sight, and when she, as very likely she did, threatened him once with the police, he struck her down. Besides, what sort of life would she have led him, once she had that hold over him? She was beginning to be troublesome enough, we know, with the hold that he had. That, at least, was a mutual hold. But I don't wonder any reference to the leather coat always shook him."

"I suppose Morris, when he met the Jenkins girl again at the Savoy, thought she was really Mrs. Robson?"

"I think so, sir. I fancy that she begged him, in quick word or two, not to give away her having worked in London and then, when she went to see him in his office, I think she told him a regular fairy tale. I would expect her to have told him that she really was an Australian girl, married to Robson, that she had run away from her husband, and had taken the name of Jenkins, and posed as an unmarried girl. But now she and her husband were reconciled, they were wealthy, and she was very happy."

"But willing to take up again with someone who had known her as 'Posey'?"

"Evidently, sir. It would not be dangerous—after that explanation. Morris, evidently, was marked for elimination when Robson learned, from the name 'Posey' on the blotting pad, that he was linked with the life in London of the woman whom Robson passed off so successfully as Annabelle Robson. Robson's only hope of holding on to that money he had now coming to him as Annabelle's husband was that there should be no suspicion that Annabelle Robson was not genuine. When I got too interested in 'Posey' he told me a cock and bull story about his wife's friend Ada Miller being so nicknamed. It was Robson, of course, who wrote the letter found beside the dead Morris."

"I bet he was sorry he worded that last note as he did. You played it for all it was worth," said his superior with a faint smile.

"I put it to Whitehouse, and to Robson, that if it wasn't suicide it must be murder. Yet, if suicide, I maintained to each that it could only, be suicide because of an attachment to Mrs. Robson, that nothing else made sense."

"Good work. Lucky for Green it was you who looked into the Morris affair. And very unlucky for Robson."

"Very lucky, sir, that Robson, who took away from the room everything which he thought might even possibly refer to Mrs. Robson, overlooked the drawer in the telephone stand, where their names among others had been entered by Morris."

"He must have had a shock when you rang him up so promptly."

"In a way I suppose so, sir. But he knew that we could not learn anything from Morris now. The man had, of course, to be silenced before the papers would have the news of the murder splashed all over their pages. Morris

would at once tell the police about Annabelle Robson
having worked in a house agent's office, as Elizabeth
Jenkins."

"But when did Robson prepare the poison? For we
cannot find any purchase by him of anything harmful?"

"I've learned that he could have had-the time, just
barely time, to have boiled aconite roots taken from The
Clearing at his new house. He was alone when he
returned there on Saturday afternoon, as it happened.
But I rather fancy the poison had been prepared some
time ago."

"From what do you gather that?"

"The first thing, or one of the first things, Robson had
done to the Grantham gardens was to have all the aconite
taken up. It looks to me, sir, as though, he had a bottle,
perhaps more than one bottle ready, should he ever want
it, and so was making quite sure that there should be
nothing in his garden to give him away. You see, I think
it's even possible that he may have prepared it for the
real Annabelle about the time she began to talk of selling
out and going home . . . Or perhaps he got it ready after
the first murder, should he need to take swift action. But
that's only guesswork. We can't prove how he got it, any
more than we can prove that he went to Morris' flat."

"We have traced three telephone calls to Morris that
Saturday evening. Two from the homes of business
acquaintances, one from a booth at King's Cross at a little
past eight, just when the train from Grantham would
have got in," said the assistant commissioner. "I think he
rang up Morris, learned that he would be in his flat, gave
as his excuse probably that he had a packet from his wife
to bring Morris."

"A book from the Grantham shelves would have
done," Pointer agreed. "I think he was admitted by
Morris, had a pleasant chat with him, handing over 'the
birthday present', and adding a bottle of 'some foreign
wine,' as he would call the liquid in the bottle. I would
further guess that he poured out a couple of tumblers, one

for his host, assuring him it was mild as milk, and must be drained at a draught. Next I should expect him to have suddenly remembered a telephone message he had promised to send, and which must go through at once, which would give him the excuse of setting his glass down on the table for a moment. I think Robson kept his hold on the telephone when Morris got ill, pretending to be ringing up a doctor, till Morris was quite incapable of moving. From the amount taken, the doctor thinks the poison would have begun to take effect within a very few minutes. Of course, all this is only theory, and Morris' death will only be mentioned, as it were, at Robson's trial."

"Quick work," said the assistant commissioner. "But then, he must have worked amazingly fast to have done what he had to do at the time of his wife's, his pseudo-wife's murder. I still don't see how he could have done it in the time, Pointer."

"If he drove all out, he could, sir. We've tried it out. He went slowly past Uthwatt, whose car he could hear a long way off, but stepped on it when out of sight."

"Did he guess what was up, do you think, when he heard that his wife had asked for the dog to be brought round?"

"It must have made him uneasy. Especially when Mr. Ash suggested, when she didn't reply, that she might be out in the garden. She had, I feel sure, just found the blood-soaked leather coat in the tin trunk, and had some suspicion of the truth. But, to continue with Robson's time table, I think he whizzed up to as near to The Clearing as he could get, raced for the house, saw his wife—to call her that—with the blood-stained coat in her hand—she screamed at him, we may be sure. He killed her, mutilating her face out of any possibility of recognition as the face of Elizabeth Jenkins, took the tin trunk back to the boxroom, forgot, or didn't see the chain and padlock, locked the bedroom door. Picked up the gun and shot Rover, and then put a shot through the crown of

his own hat—rammed the leather coat of his first victim
into the stove after first dashing plenty of paraffin on it.
It didn't need to be burned up, only to have the blood
stains undetectable, put the 60 pounds given his wife
back into his pocket, and ran shouting out to meet
Uthwatt, to continue the play as he had devised it."

"When did you first see the whole triple murder
clearly—consecutively—as it were? I say 'when' but I
really mean 'how' as well."

"Well, sir, when I heard that Acland had an alibi for
the hours during, before, and after Mrs. Robson's murder,
I could not see that he had any thing on which to
blackmail either Green or Whitehouse, the two accepted
candidates for the post of murderer. It wasn't as if both of
them, or all three of them, to include Robson, the other
man known to have been on the premises, hadn't been
staying at The Clearing, so that the chance of possession
of something from the scene of the crime wouldn't mean
anything. The only hold Acland could have had over any
of them was to have actually seen them during the time
of the crime at the house. That, the rector proved to have
been impossible."

"Then why was Acland killed? He was a blackmailer,
all who really knew him said, and his record bore this
out."

"Killed to stop him blackmailing, yes, but for
something else than The Clearing murder, yet probably
linked with it, for it was evidently The Clearing that
made blackmail possible. Something he knew that would
logically point to the murderer was how I now read
Acland's power. Something in the past— Then, on the
same day as I heard of his alibi, came evidence which
pointed to Robson as the murderer. Uthwatt said that
when he rushed through the house with the seemingly
distraught husband, the door of the boxroom was locked.

"Now the door is very lightly hung on its hinges. A
push would have burst it open, but Robson told him it
was only an empty boxroom, and not to stop. His rush

was so infectious, that Uthwatt, without another word, ran on with him. It was the police who had the door unlocked, and found the cupboard, as Robson had said, empty. They didn't think enough of it to mention it in their report. But would any husband, hot on the track of the murderer of his wife, lying below, have let a locked boxroom pass without investigating it? Never!"

"I see the point. I agree," said the assistant commissioner slowly, "but go on, go over your reasoning step by step."

"As soon as I heard that, I knew only the murderer himself could have known for certain that the cupboard was empty. Only the murderer, acting the part of a searcher, would have vouched for it like that, passed it by twice. Once when he himself, according to his own account, ran over the house, the second time with Uthwatt. Acland was killed by the same hand that killed Mrs. Robson, we all agreed. So Robson was in danger of blackmail for what? Not for the murder of his wife, except by sure and certain inference of something known to Acland, for I had learned that Acland could not have seen Robson kill her. Something in the past, another crime, of course. This immediately raised the question—had Mrs. Robson too, come on traces of that crime? Her death, so apparently unfortunate for Robson, was it the lesser of two evils? That meant was there anything she could have discovered in his past which would have sent him up for a long term of penal servitude? It would have to be a very long term for him to throw overboard a huge fortune, as he did when he killed her. In all his life there was no evidence, no connection to link with any such crime. Yet it would only have been for knowledge of what would mean his certain and sure life sentence, that he would have silenced her. A previous murder? His hands are violent hands. The burnt coat, which was proven to have come from Australia . . . the dog sent for by Mrs. Robson . . . the coat which had a button pulled off it in some violent struggle, a struggle only for the coat, according to all reports of the room . . . the charred fragments tested, showed that a great deal of blood had been on the coat . . . the boxroom that Robson always kept locked . . . I suppose that Mrs. Robson, thinking her husband was away till the next day, had decided to have a look in the boxroom and into that tin trunk? I think we shall find that she had both keys cut from Robson's key without his knowledge, her curiosity having been roused by the door and the trunk, being both always kept locked. Now, supposing, she had come on traces of a previous murder, Robson would have had to silence her at once. With this idea, everything fitted, Mrs. Robson wanted the dog to track down where the body that had been in the blood-stained coat was hidden, if it was on the premises. The padlock and chain were around that tin trunk, I fancy. Acland had some notion of a first murder, and so felt certain that Robson had killed his wife to prevent her giving him away. Mrs. Robson, before she was silenced, yet sent a message, when she wrote on a flyleaf, *In memory of Posey*, and sent the book off to a man in town whom she had met again after an interval, a couple of months before her death. Only when Robson saw the flyleaf was Morris in danger, for Robson kept the book and had a look at it. Because of the marks recorded on the blotting sheet. Evidently the name *Posey* came out clearly. So then Posey was, I believed, connected with the first murder too, and because of the connection, Morris had to die. A very slight reason, I grant, but the crushed face fitted in here. For that destruction there could only be one reason, barring the very improbable one of some great hatred venting its spite on the woman just struck down. That reason was to prevent, identification. But there was no effort to prevent identification as Annabelle Robson. Was it to prevent identification as Posey? Who was Posey then? Someone known to Mrs. Robson and to Morris . . . someone out of her past? Her past, investigate it, fine-comb it, riddle it, as we might, yielded nothing except one important fact. She seemed to dread meeting

Morris when she had been in town, recovering from her breakdown, according to her husband.

"You see, sir, Whitehouse's signed statement misled me for all this time. In it he says that Annabelle Bigger was seventeen when he last saw her in Canberra.It seems that he first wrote eleven and then corrected that to seven, and the constable typing the copy read the age as seventeen, and Whitehouse never noticed the slip when he signed the page. Now, if she had been seventeen and he met her again when she was twenty three, impersonation, or substitution, was almost impossible. I could not understand the case except by the assumption, in spite of Whitehouse's statement, that the Annabelle Robson murdered at The Clearing was not the Annabelle of Canberra. Assume that, and everything become logical. The first Mrs. Robson had been killed and buried, the second was to pass as the real one. When Whitehouse took over The Clearing, Robson put in a bathroom for him, and built the little greenhouse, as well as adding a porch over the front door."

"Skilful idea," said the assistant commissioner. "He did everything himself?"

"All except the porch. The greenhouse, with its cement floor, made an ideal hiding place for any body. When Whitehouse arrived at Thoresway, I think the real Annabelle had just been buried, after being murdered in the heat of some fierce quarrel—perhaps she wanted to get her money back and go home. Possibly too, Robson knew that Zilla Ash was infatuated with him, that she had quite a nice little sum of money, and would hand it over to him without a word. I'm afraid that may have had something to do with the first murder."

"Useful way that bomb exploded against the glasshouse, at The Clearing," said the assistant commissioner. "The kind that blows up and not down, so that it merely cracked the cement floor, and cleared off the upper, structure . . . one of our own British bombs, I'm told."

"Dropped by accident evidently," said Pointer, blandly. "As you say, sir, it helped us to get the body out before Robson could get hold of it as he meant to. That air raid was very opportune for him, he must have thought . . . once fling out those bones into some other place, well hidden among undergrowth, and, when found, if found long afterwards, they would be thought to have been some victim of the Nazis."

"Yes. I understand you asked the chief, constable to see to it that the Clearing should be picketed throughout the night; and the Home Guard were told to look out for someone claiming to be Robson the owner, who would try to act the part of a fifth columnist, or even a Nazi agent, or a parachutist. They were delighted at the tip, and arrested Robson as soon as he set foot on his own land. Going back a bit, I suppose the dog was shot so as to be on the safe side?"

"I think that was why Robson bought him in the first place, sir. To take him away from the neighborhood. But having brought him to The Clearing, he had to kill him."

"You think Acland knew the truth?"

"He had some inkling of the facts, I believe. Robson himself said he once read his thoughts. Robson said it was in regard to his wife's wreath, but I think that was the moment when Robson decided Acland must go."

"The 'two women' connected with 'the button', the 'blood all around' must all have been a bit trying for Robson," murmured the other.

"Acland either really had a touch of second sight, as the local superintendent half believes, or had also unlocked the boxroom, and looked into the locked and padlocked trunk. Anyway, he was dangerous, and Robson must have been delighted when he got the idea to kill him in such a way that Green could be caught red-handed for his murder, and so for the murder of the so-called Annabelle Robson. Acland, of course, was killed before Robson went down to the village for tobacco."

"But how did Robson manage the screech?"

"He was in the village at the time of the screech all right, sir. But you can get a really blood-curdling howl by inserting a cracked tiny rubber ball high up in any water tap. The screech—I've tried it out—comes after a length of time, depending on how far up the pipe it has been thrust, the water carries it down little by little, and it is when it gets near the outlet that the noise comes, and the ball, with a last scream drops out and rolls away."

"Supposing Acland hadn't gone on down to Hawkstone, would the tiger have been without any kill?"

"I have an idea, nothing to go on, that Miss Ash might have been lured down, if Acland hadn't arrived."

"Miss Ash? I thought she was in love with Robson?"

"At one time she undoubtedly was, but of late somehow she makes him uncomfortable whenever she's mentioned. She suspects something, I think—or possibly even knows something—which was why, in my opinion, she tried so hard to get Whitehouse away. And I think she was very shrewd to join the A.T.S. when she did. Of course, we shall have to have a talk with her at once!"

"You've not heard how she was killed?"

"Zilla Ash? No sir."

"Last night. In the big raid over Hull. Not far from her A.T.S. convoy were some ammunition trucks hidden in a wood. The four drivers took refuge in a ditch, which got a direct hit. Zilla's officer was killed too. She took command of her section. Ordered the girls to a safer place—and saw to it that they went. Then she herself drove out the trucks, one by one, from the burning wood. She got them, all four, clear, by a miracle of unhurried, good driving, and what we call luck, though the canvas of the last truck was afire as she drove it out. And then, when it was all over, she was hit by a fragment from a bomb that fell quite a distance away. Killed outright. The least we can do is to keep her name out of all this."

Pointer agreed. There was a moment's silence. Well, to him, something in the face of Zilla Ash suggested that a brave death would have been what she would have chosen.

The telephone rang. A letter had just arrived by a taxi for the chief inspector. It came from a well-known solicitor in London, and was marked 'Urgent'. Re Annabelle Robson, decd. Pointer and the assistant commissioner looked at each other. "Send, it up at once," ordered the latter, and in a moment Pointer was handed a long envelope. Inside was another long envelope and a note which ran:

Dear Sir,

Miss Ash came to us last week, and directed us, should her death, whether by enemy action or not, take place before the trial of a man called Green for the murder of Acland, to send on to you the enclosed envelope marked as directed. We are doing this now, and should like a receipt in due course from you of its safe arrival.

Faithfully yours,
Dodson & Royce.

Pointer opened the enclosed envelope on which in a clear, but straggling woman's hand, his name had been written.

Dear Mister Pointer,
It is very unlikely that this letter will ever be handed to you, but even if it is, please only use it if Green is in danger of being hanged for what I feel sure he did not do.
Harold Robson killed his wife, so he probably killed Acland too. I saw Harold Robson standing at his bedroom window after firing the second shot and leaning well out to look all 'around before putting the rifle away. He pretended to me that it was someone

else who must have made himself up to look like him and, for the moment, he half convinced me. But it was Harold Robson himself, all right. As I felt, however, that I was partly or muchly to blame for his having killed his wife, I said nothing. I loved him at that time, and thought he was in love with me. But he was not, and the more I thought it over the less I liked it—and him. Why did he shoot Rover? And when he talked of Green and Whitehouse and of peril, I began to think that if there was any danger it would come from Harold Robson. So I got Mr. Whitehouse away. I think that Acland too thought Robson was the murderer. I knew Acland of course at first sight just as Harold Robson must have, and wanted Acland to come away too but he had come down for the purpose of watching Robson. He felt quite secure because Green was in the house too, and, because he was certain that Robson had not recognized him. I did not see Robson at Hawkstone, but Acland said he was there.

I am sure if I read. this over, I should write it quite differently, so I am closing it up at once.

I am taking it to my mother's family lawyer, and shall ask him to keep it, and only send it to you should anything happen to me before Green's trial, for of course I shall come forward then, and tell what I know.

Sincerely yours,
Zilla Ash.

P.S.—I did throw the leather coat away, the morning of the murder. I can't think how he got hold of it.

The two men reading laid the letter down on the table between them. "Determined to stay on. Of course, with Green there, Acland would think he was quite safe in putting the screw on Robson, putting it on hard," said the assistant commissioner. "But how long would you have given Miss Ash—supposing you had not caught Robson?"

Pointer was folding up Zilla Ash's letter. "The leather coat given her by the so-called Annabelle Robson was evidently one that Robson must have bought for Miss Jenkins to bring down with her, so as to look like her predecessor. The original one must have been overlooked when he buried his wife's body, and he kept it locked up as it was difficult to destroy. He felt quite safe, once the Jenkins girl had been accepted as genuine, and a leather coat, drenched with blood, is difficult to destroy.

"Miss Ash was a bit off the truth when she thought Whitehouse was in danger from him. Robson, of course, was keen on getting him away from Green before Green should have milked him dry. I think Robson hoped that Whitehouse would do just what he has proposed to do, that is, share the Australian fortune with him. Well, this letter won't be needed. But I'm glad she wrote it, "and Pointer placed it with the other papers marked "Re Annabelle Robson, Deceased."

THE END

Other Resurrected Press Books in *The Chief Inspector Pointer Mystery Series*

AVAILABLE FROM RESURRECTED PRESS!

THE EDWARDIAN DETECTIVES
LITERARY SLEUTHS OF THE EDWARDIAN ERA

The exploits of the great Victorian Detectives, Poe's C. Auguste Dupin, Gaboriau's Lecoq, and most famously, Arthur Conan Doyle's Sherlock Holmes, are well known. But what of those fictional detectives that came after, those of the Edwardian Age? The period between the death of Queen Victoria and the First World War had been called the Golden Age of the detective short story, but how familiar is the modern reader with the sleuths of this era? And such an extraordinary group they were, including in their numbers an unassuming English priest, a blind man, a master of disguises, a lecturer in medical jurisprudence, a noble woman working for Scotland Yard, and a savant so brilliant he was known as "The Thinking Machine."

To introduce readers to these detectives, Resurrected Press has assembled a collection of stories featuring these and other remarkable sleuths in The Edwardian Detectives.

- The Case of Laker, Absconded by Arthur Morrison
- The Fenchurch Street Mystery by Baroness Orczy
- The Crime of the French Café by Nick Carter
- The Man with Nailed Shoes by R Austin Freeman
- The Blue Cross by G. K. Chesterton
- The Case of the Pocket Diary Found in the Snow by Augusta Groner
- The Ninescore Mystery by Baroness Orczy
- The Riddle of the Ninth Finger by Thomas W. Hanshew
- The Knight's Cross Signal Problem by Ernest Bramah

- The Problem of Cell 13 by Jacques Futrelle
- The Conundrum of the Golf Links by Percy James Brebner
- The Silkworms of Florence by Clifford Ashdown
- The Gateway of the Monster by William Hope Hodgson
- The Affair at the Semiramis Hotel by A. E. W. Mason
- The Affair of the Avalanche Bicycle & Tyre Co., LTD by Arthur Morrison

RESURRECTED PRESS CLASSIC MYSTERY CATALOGUE

Journeys into Mystery
Travel and Mystery in a More Elegant Time

The Edwardian Detectives
Literary Sleuths of the Edwardian Era

Gems of Mystery
Lost Jewels from a More Elegant Age

E. C. Bentley
Trent's Last Case: The Woman in Black

Ernest Bramah
Max Carrados Resurrected:
The Detective Stories of Max Carrados

Agatha Christie
The Secret Adversary
The Mysterious Affair at Styles

Octavus Roy Cohen
Midnight

Freeman Wills Croft
The Ponson Case
The Pit Prop Syndicate

J. S. Fletcher
The Herapath Property
The Rayner-Slade Amalgamation
The Chestermarke Instinct
The Paradise Mystery
Dead Men's Money

Louis Tracy
The Strange Case of Mortimer Fenley
The Albert Gate Mystery
The Bartlett Mystery
The Postmaster's Daughter
The House of Peril
The Sandling Case: What Would You Have Done?
Charles Edmonds Walk
The Paternoster Ruby

John R. Watson
The Mystery of the Downs
The Hampstead Mystery

Edgar Wallace
The Daffodil Mystery
The Crimson Circle

Carolyn Wells
Vicky Van
The Man Who Fell Through the Earth
In the Onyx Lobby
Raspberry Jam
The Clue
The Room with the Tassels
The Vanishing of Betty Varian
The Mystery Girl
The White Alley
The Curved Blades
Anybody but Anne
The Bride of a Moment
Faulkner's Folly
The Diamond Pin
The Gold Bag
The Mystery of the Sycamore
The Come Backy

Raoul Whitfield
Death in a Bowl

And much more!
Visit ResurrectedPress.com
for our complete catalogue

About Resurrected Press

A division of Intrepid Ink, LLC, Resurrected Press is dedicated to bringing high quality, vintage books back into publication. See our entire catalogue and find out more at www.ResurrectedPress.com.

About Intrepid Ink, LLC

Intrepid Ink, LLC provides full publishing services to authors of fiction and non-fiction books, eBooks and websites. From editing to formatting, from publishing to marketing, Intrepid Ink gets your creative works into the hands of the people who want to read them. Find out more at www.IntrepidInk.com.